Sieged

Kyuka Lilymjok

ISBN 978-978-069-686-3

Published by:
Free Pen Publishers
10 Lachlan Close, Maitama, Abuja

Any people depicted in stock imagery provided by Thinkstock are models, and such images are being used for such purposes only.

This book is printed on acid-free paper.

To my wife Maria and my children: Justice,
Sunfair and Fairprincess

Swords are never far from the camp of
injustice

Chapter One

The train rattled and jangled on the railtrack like a one-legged cripple propped up by a metal stick hurtling home to escape a gathering rainstorm. By the railtrack were many party and non-party enthusiasts waving excitedly at the passing train. By one of the open doors of the train stood Jamimi the primehead candidate of the Peoples Liberation Movement (PLM) waving enthusiastically at the people standing by the railtrack. On top of the train and hanging on door handles were many party supporters really having a party on the train, if their shouts of excitement and maniacal waving of hands and swinging of legs were anything to go by.

Most of the people by the railtrack waving excitedly at the train as it made its passage through them were seeing a train for the first time in their lives. Most of the people on and in the train were travelling by train for the first time in their lives. Those who had seen a moving train before, out of nostalgia, appeared more excited than those who had not. For decades, the railtracks of Bivan's house had not been plied by any train. Most of the trains that used to ply the railtracks were more than three hundred years old and therefore no longer rail worthy. Age and lack of maintenance had over the years worn out the trains until there was no train left to ply the railtracks which themselves were sagging and creaking under the weight of age.

Jamimi who saw rail transportation as a viable alternative and complement to road transportation watched the gradual disappearance of the trains from the railtracks with dismay and rising anger. He could not understand how successive governments in Bivan's house could sit by watching rail transportation winding up like a winding sheet in a coffin or grave without doing anything. When he joined party politics and was nominated the primehead candidate of the Peoples Liberation Movement, he decided to campaign for election by train as a token of what he would do if he becomes primehead. Also apart from the fact that he thought a train campaign would be cheaper, he wanted to give literal meaning to the metaphor of a campaign train, which had become a sobriquet for a campaign convoy in Bivan's house.

The train was branded with the pictures of Jamimi the party's primehead candidate. It was also branded with the logo of the party and its flag. It was an old train that the party refurbished for its campaign. The moment Jamimi made the suggestion of using the rail for the campaign instead of the road, many people liked the idea more by the sheer force of its novelty than by any visible benefits of such means of mobilizing a campaign. But when the campaign commenced with the train, those who initially could not see the benefits of a train campaign began to do so. On the first day of using the train, as they rumbled through the town of Bangora, virtually the whole town was by the railtrack to behold the train.

Myth had it that the origin of politics in Bivan's house was different from its origin elsewhere. According to myth, politics in Bivan's house originated from a society of headhunters. The leader of the society of headhunters was called the primehead and so he who was called president or prime minister in other countries came to be called primehead in Bivan's house and what was called national assembly or parliament in other countries was called the house of archery in Bivan's house. A governor was the big feast, ministers were ceremonial feasts, ambassadors were close banquets, commissioners were ceremonial pots, local government chairmen were common calabashes and councillors were hunting bags. Like butchers said to have started surgery, myth had it that headhunters started politics in Bivan's house. From its headhunting ancestry, politics in Bivan's house was to later graduate into a game played by people of the streets.

At the time Jamimi joined politics, politics in Bivan's house was largely played by street people who had no job because they were not educated or trained for one. In Bivan's house if you had failed at everything, if no one could engage you in any job because you were not qualified for any, you joined politics. When asked what his occupation was, a person without training and skills said politics as if politics were a profession like painting or bricklaying. Milling around street corners, idling about street intersections and waterfronts, yawning and sighing out of boredom and hunger, street people with street manners ganged up to play politics the way they played games on the streets. Long before he joined politics, Jamimi had discussed the street character of politics and politicians in Bivan's house with a colleague in his office.

'It seems to me,' said Jamimi, 'that while schools are giving certificates to those who attend them and acquire learning and skills so that they can go find decent jobs, the street is giving certificates to those who have been long on it and had imbibed its culture and values to enter politics.'

'You are just saying it now,' said the colleague. 'A motor park tout from my village now in politics had long said something similar to me. He said to survive and prosper in politics, one had to be certified fit for it by the street. It was not such *siriri werere* – an all-comers affair as one might think. He said he did not join politics until he was certified fit by the street to do so.'

'Wonderful!' exclaimed Jamimi. 'So what struck me is not an eccentric brainwave but the reality of our situation. The street giving certificates in politics to layabouts!'

That's the situation,' intoned the colleague. 'The street gives certificates to those that had served it well to join politics. The highway robber, the street urchin, the prostitute, the violent gang member, they are all practitioners of the street who the street licenses to practise politics.'

'Since demons are also known to walk the streets, I presume they also receive these certificates from the street.'

'There is no doubt about that.'

Jamimi had not always been a politician. He began to develop interest in politics while working as a director in the ministry of commerce and industry. Politicians - people without much education and much experience, were appointed ceremonial feasts over him and relied on him to do the job while they took the credit. Bad as that was, it did not anger him like the politicians' lack of interest in planning and executing projects that would improve the lot of the people. All they were interested in was ambushing public funds for themselves and political layabouts they used as thugs during electioneering campaigns and during elections. These political hangers-on trooped to various offices every working day, begging, sometimes demanding as of right patronage and bonanza for their support that made the attainment of the office possible for the political office holder. He was particularly irked one day when a political thug told the ceremonial feast of his ministry to his face that the office he was holding was like a gourd of palm wine that was jointly purchased. Usually when a gourd of palm wine was jointly purchased, it was given to one of the number that purchased it to share. The person sharing could not because the gourd was between his legs claim ownership of it more than any of the number that purchased it. Seeking to etch his point more deeply, he said the office the ceremonial feast was occupying was the dead body of an elephant he, the ceremonial feast, and other hunters killed. As such, he was entitled whenever he was without meat to come with his knife and cut. The ceremonial feast was merely a custodian of the elephant for all the hunters and has no more interest in it than any other hunter that killed it.

The thug's comparison of the office of the ceremonial feast with that of a mere custodian of an elephant a group of hunters had killed evoked memories of the headhunting origin of politics in Bivan's house. Allusions to occasions when politics in Bivan's house was exclusively practiced by headhunters and the continuous use of headhunters' titles for political office holders at a time when politics had moved substantially from headhunters to people of the street was what kept politics in Bivan's house sandwiched between headhunting and the waywardness of the street.

Because of the quality of people engaged in politics in Bivan's house, government was not seen as an agency of public service, but of *eating* public money. Once, someone who saw government as an agency of service was appointed ceremonial feast and he began complaining about lack of performance by the government that appointed him. Another ceremonial feast who saw his own appointment as an invitation to come and *eat* lashed out at the ceremonial feast who was complaining: 'You have been invited to come and *eat* and you are talking; don't you know in Africa talking while eating is bad table manners?'

The complaining ceremonial feast said he did not know that his appointment was an invitation to *eat* and that if government was all about *eating*, then government may as well close its door and hang on the outside knob a notice that reads: SILENCE! EATING IN PROGRESS.

The mental picture Jamimi had was that politicians had barricaded themselves inside government *eating*. Those outside government were dealing blows and kicks on the door shouting to be let in. They also wanted to *eat*. In the end it was the *eating* mentality of

Bivan's house politicians that finally angered him into joining politics to add his kick and blow on the locked door. He started with labor union politics and rose to become the national president of Bivan's house labor association. It was from there he joined the Peoples Liberation Movement, which nominated him as its primehead candidate.

Chapter Two

Those who knew Jamimi as a student in the university were shocked to see him in politics. As a student, Jamimi was studious, quiet and apolitical. He was never part of any students' politics either as an aspirant for office or a partisan for any aspirant. During students' election week when the stirrings and bubbles of youth were called forth like the froth of over fermented palmwine by the alluring blink of power to enliven the campus, Jamimi was an island of still waters unaffected by the gaiety and fanfare going on around him. At such times, he was either in the library reading or in his room doing the same thing. Alone at study, he did not seem to have any boring moment. On his face were to be seen different shades of expression of pleasure as he, in the words of his classmate, *ate up all the knowledge piled up in the books of the library.* One day he was reading in his room while his room-mate Nkume and their common friend Bobi were eating *eba.* They had invited him several times to join them, but it seemed he was too possessed by the book he was reading, to join them.

'Professor!' said Bobi. 'There you are *eating* books and we are here eating *eba*; feeding your mind while we feed our *gizzards*. Softly, softly before you run out of eyes in your youth. Books *eat* eyes as eyes *eat* books if you don't know.'

'Someone told me it is *eba* that *eats* up the eyes,' Jamimi said, closing the book he was reading. 'So, you may be out of eyes sooner than I.'

'Whoever started this rumor must have quarreled with a cassava farmer and is out to ruin him,' said Bobi. 'These kinds of rumors are everywhere these days. Someone told me that eating too much of groundnut oil takes away a man's potency. What can be more scary?'

'Every industry in this country has closed down except the rumor mill,' said Nkume. 'Instead of closing down or downsizing, it is expanding at a time other industries had run out of raw materials.'

'The more other industries run out of raw materials, the more the rumor mill gets raw materials,' said Jamimi. 'The idle hands laid off by the closing industries must find something to engage them. That something is idle talk. The loss of the industry is the gain of the rumor mill.'

'Prof, Prof!' exclaimed Bobi, clenching his two hands into fists with the thumbs sticking out, folding and stretching his hand in salute of what Jamimi had said. 'Whenever you open your mouth to talk, the books you have *eaten* keep tumbling out.'

'It is not only when he opens his mouth to talk that a book falls out,' said Nkume. 'Even when he yawns, belches or sneezes, something bookish splashes on me. I am his roommate. I should know. The guy reads too much. This morning when I returned from the campaign rounds for Chakko our candidate for the presidency of the students' union, he was still reading. And do you know what time I returned? 4 o'clock in the morning. I left him in the room 8 o'clock in the evening reading and I returned 4 o'clock in the morning and met him still reading. Bobi, calculate the time he read yesterday and today for us.'

'I wasn't reading when you returned,' protested Jamimi. I was only thumbing through the book.'

'I caught you red-handed; so don't deny it,' said Nkume.

They all laughed.

'You caught me red handed, was I stealing?' Jamimi repeated to himself still laughing.

'Yes, you were; but you were stealing from your own farm,' said Nkume with a mischievous gleam on his face. 'You are too often seen poring into books that you are sometimes embarrassed when you are found guzzling one more.'

'Politics is walking about the campus shaking everybody's hand said Bobi. 'You are the only one keeping your hand behind you denying *our lord the friend and fiend* a handshake.'

'What are you saying Bobi?' asked Nkume. 'Is it a matter of keeping his hands behind him or the whole of him out of the view of politics? When politics is walking round the campus, he is either in the library *biting* the books or in this room *chewing* them.'

'Jamimi, what you fail to understand is that if we end up having a religious fundamentalist as our student leader, even these books you are reading, you may not be able to read them again,' said Bobi.

'Why?'

'He may pass a *law* saying we should devote more time to God and prayers than to our books since heaven is all that matters to them. And from what I can see of you, it is this world that matters to you. I have never seen you reading a religious book. For that matter, have I ever seen you pray? Can you now see it is not politic for you to avoid politics?'

'When religion makes promises of heaven and hell, it provides the madness that will subvert men's reason and senses,' said Bobi. 'Brahma the Indian god that does not make promises of heaven and hell to his devotees, no one is fanatical about him. Very few people pray to him and there are few shrines for him. But, not the other gods. They want big shrines and want to be prayed to even if they give nothing or don't even exist. That to me is fraud.'

'You are charging gods with fraud?' said Nkume shrinking his body in mocked revulsion. 'That's a piece of blasphemy I pray does not reach heaven. Thankfully this room is padded. You may not be heard in heaven.'

'You are assuming there is a God somewhere,' said Bobi. 'Well, let's leave gods alone and talk about the important issue of politics and why Jamimi must have interest in it. Prof, more than any of us, you know the saying that *evil prospers when good men stay away from society and do nothing*. If liberals or free thinkers like us stay away from politics, the religious fanatics will take over and say that everyone must think like them. They may even say every man must wear a *beard* or a *cross*, and every woman *niqab* – a dress that creates a society of masquerades.'

'You have said something there perhaps without knowing it,' said Jamimi, breaking his silence. 'The *niqab* creates masquerades that haunt and hypocrites that irritate. Whenever I see a woman in that wear that turns her into a moving grove, I wonder what she is thinking or if she even has any brains to think.'

'What's the goldmine the *niqab* seeks to secure?'

'Ask them Bobi, ask them.'

'Yet, if we don't get involved in politics, it is absurdities like the *niqab* we would be inviting into this university,' said Nkume. 'Fanatics in power may even provoke a crisis that would lead to the closure of the school. Remember how a year ago the school was closed for three months because of a clash between Moslem and Christian fanatics.'

'The crisis you speak of, if my memory still serves me, was precipitated by the leaderships of the two faiths,' said Jamimi. 'As far as I am concerned, crises in society are provoked by authorities of whatever kind. If there were no associations such as the Christian Students Vanguard or the Moslem Students League, there would not have been the crisis you speak of. Wherever you find associations or governments of whatever kind, there is mischief in their midst. I believe mischief even motivates their formation. Associations and governments exist to make demands on people and people resent being demanded of. The solution to crises in the world therefore lies in disbanding governments and associations. I am sure you can both recall the peace we enjoyed on this campus during the two years there was no students unionism in the university. Associations and governments to me are cults preying on society. Away with them and you can depend more on order.'

'But they won't go away, Prof,' screeched Bobi. 'That's the problem. Government is like the *loyan* weed in the farmers' farm. The *loyan* weed attaches itself so intimately to the crop that the farmer cannot easily pull it out without pulling out his crop. The stream might be better off without the mermaid, but is it easy to chase the mermaid out of the stream? In my village, mermaids were kept in streams by witches and sorcerers and could only be removed from the stream by those who put them there. If we cannot chase away the mermaid from the stream because we didn't put it there, why don't we put our own mermaid in the stream, even if it means us becoming witches and sorcerers?'

'I am afraid I cannot be a friend of your views nor buy them with what I least regard because they stand in the way of what I set my eyes upon. Governments and politics are all about folly and deceit. I am grieved by deceit and not entertained by folly. I can only partake of politics to my unhappiness. In my mouth, I carry neither the water of folly nor the fire of deceit that are the fuel needed to galvanize the political machine and send it into orbit. What I set my eyes upon is scholarship: to see what is before me, but ignorance will not allow me see; to hear what nature whispers in the dark and understand what is beyond common knowledge.'

Up to the time Jamimi left university, he did not become a partisan of politics. He graduated with a second class, upper division degree and was the best student of his class. By convention, he should have been retained as a graduate assistant if he wanted to. He wanted to, but could not be retained because he was not a Kunsu the majority tribe of Bivan's house. Neither was he a Moslem the favored religion of the eastern part of Bivan's house. His desire was to lecture in the university and become a professor one day. Already as a student he was called professor by his classmates. He wanted to become one to fulfill the prophecy of his classmates, if their nicknaming him professor was a prophecy. That he would teach in the university and become a professor was partly the reason he read so hard to graduate with a class of degree that would actualize that dream for him. Having not been retained by his *alma mater* situated in his home state, he applied to other universities of Bivan's house, but they kept turning him away asking him why he could not be employed by his *alma mater* which as it were was located in his state of origin. For six years, he laid siege on a university job without finding any. At the end of the sixth year of searching for the job of his choice without finding it, his father who had fended for him died and he had now to fend for himself. It was then hunger laid siege on him. He quickly found a job in a secondary school where he taught for five years. Teaching in a secondary school he found privation and ignorance stalking him. Books were what he needed most, but his salary could barely feed him and so he had no money to buy books. Even if he had the money, there were hardly books of general interest in the bookshops for him to buy.

Bookshops sold only books that were recommended for one examination or the other. There were no general reading materials in the bookshops because once out of school, a member of Bivan's house did not see the sense in reading again. Since bookshops are in a business of buying and selling, they only bought and sold commodities patronized by their customers and these were mostly recommended texts for secondary school and university students. The few members of Bivan's house who still read after school bought their books abroad when they travelled out or asked their friends and acquaintances travelling abroad to do so for them if they could not travel themselves. While classical books were missing in the country's libraries, the latest cars in the world were everywhere on the nation's streets.

As a student, Jamimi had always sat down to contemplate the attitudes of members of Bivan's house to knowledge and material things. Knowledge was only useful if it would win a material thing. Nothing in

Jamimi's mind captured the attitude of members of Bivan's house than the words of Jonathan's father to his son in Jonathan Kingston Seagull: *If you must study, study food and how to get it. This flying business is all very well, but you can't eat a glide you know. Don't you forget that the reason you fly is to eat.* Reading for *eating*, members of Bivan's house had traded the life of an eagle, which requires thought, for the life of a seagull, which is all about eating, farting and defecating. In childish admiration of the toys that ideas delivered, Bivan's house members were scoffing ideas and longing for toys. To him, this was an infantile mentality. He said so to Bobi one afternoon when they were sitting under a tree, enjoying a reprieve from the blistering sun that was escorting them from their class to the hostel.

'How on earth can you characterize your people in such derogatory terms?' said Bobi, in mock anger.

'Well, this is how I see it,' said Jamimi. 'It is only infants that are over-excited with toys. Cable satellite came with a variety of channels beaming assorted films, Bivan's house members abandoned books. Cell phones came, Bivan's house members abandoned landlines. Email came and we abandoned the post office. Right now our post offices are holes for rats and snakes.'

Out of school, Jamimi was seeing more of the infantile behavior of Bivan's house members. Whenever he lamented the blight, he was ridiculed as one full of sour grapes. He would amass more toys and have no regard for knowledge if he had money he was always told whenever he complained of people's obsession with luxury goods instead of seeking knowledge. He joined politics partly because he wanted to prove that he was different.

After working for six years in the secondary school, Jamimi moved to the Ministry of Commerce and Industry and from there to the plastic industry. It was in the plastic industry he became the president of Bivan's house national labor union. When he retired from the plastic industry, he joined politics and was made the primehead candidate of the Peoples Liberation Movement.

Chapter Three

Merima made his way through a choking crowd of people to the podium where he was to address a political rally feeling little of the excitement of the noisy crowd that was hired to give pomp and pageantry to the political rally. Heat leaking from the sun was eating his eyes like steam. Despite the baking sun, he was wearing a big gown, when even without a shirt on, the heat would still have been baking enough. But he had no choice in the matter. He was a politician and could only dress the way he was if he meant to have by him the respectability and regard of the office he was seeking.

Merima was the primehead candidate for the ruling United Action Congress (UAC) which Jamimi's Peoples Liberation Movement was trying to wrest power from. As Merima walked towards the podium, he was wondering what he would tell the people. Whatever he said was going to sound hollow- as hollow as an old cow horn without even its musical notes. Most of the people at the rally were idle people and he was going to the podium to give an idle talk to them. The air around him was hot and whatever he would say on that podium was going to be a lot of hot air to him and the crowd that would cheer and hiss at what he would say. There is nothing as wretched as lying knowing the person to whom you are lying knows you are lying and you lying know he knows you are lying. To complete the exasperating picture of his pathetic condition, this charade was altogether unnecessary to his becoming the primehead of Bivan's house. He would be the primehead of Bivan's house even if no one in the country voted for him; for that matter he was not even sure his wife would vote for him. She kept prevaricating in her support for him. When she thought she could be first lady, she was full of support for him. When she thought she might lose the spotlight of first lady to his mistress, she withdrew her support. If the spotlight would not beam on her head why should it on another woman? Nothing would be more sapping to her sense of self-worth or galling to her demand for reward than such an eventuality.

As he moved through the crowd to the podium, he was greeted with *si ko mee du* by the rented crowd. *Si ko mee du* was the most popular political slogan used by supporters of different candidates seeking election into any political office. It meant the candidate must occupy the office he was seeking. It was both a prayer for victory and a threat to anyone who tried to scuttle that victory. However, most of the people that shouted *si ko mee du* hardly supported any candidate or even belonged to any political party. They were mostly layabouts who shouted *si ko mee du* to a candidate hoping he would give them money. On election day, most of them did not go near any polling unit to vote. When he first joined politics and contested for a seat in his state's house of archery, he took *si ko mee du* to be an expression of support, but quickly found it was not when during campaign he was shocked to find that someone who had been shouting *si ko mee du* repeatedly to him was neither a member of his party nor his supporter but a member of *si ko mee du* which was an association of sort.

'You mean you are not a member of UAC?' he had asked the man.

'I am not in any political party,' the man had answered, unabashed. 'I am a *si ko mee du* member.'

'Is *si ko mee du* an association or what?'

'Yes, it is an association with a chairman, a secretary and all the other officers of an association.'

Three days after this exchange a corpse was being conveyed from the mortuary to the burial ground and some members of *si ko mee du* mistaking the funeral procession for a campaign convoy started shouting *si ko mee du*.

Today's rally was taking place in Gazumba Square located at the heart of Hamze town. The podium was at the center of the square. It was constructed with wood and covered with a tarpaulin. Flying over the podium were the flags of the United Action Congress and the national flag of Bivan's house. Both the party flags and the national flag looked soiled. The national flag in particular looked like it was dragged on the ground from wherever to the square. The party flags looked so old and worn out as to seem rag-torn. The sun, the wind and the rain had bitten them and each of these elements of the weather had left its teeth where it had bitten the flags.

Merima was now under the flags and was bellowing, 'UAC!'

'Power!' the crowd roared.

'UAC!'

'Power!'

The silence that followed the people's deafening shout of 'power!' was so pressing as to be almost physical. In the silence, a lone voice of protest like a quill from a crouching porcupine rose and hit Merima on his forehead: 'The more the people are given power the more impotent they become!'

'That's one of the ironies of Bivan's house!' cried another voice before Merima could recover from the embarrassment and regain his dignity. 'Beside this political irony, there is the religious irony. People attend church and mosque religiously, but behave irreligiously outside the church and mosque. Then there is the economic and social irony. There is so much wealth in Bivan's house, but people are so poor that they don't have where to hang themselves. The political slogan of UAC the ruling party is power, yet there is no electric power in Bivan's house. The entire nation feeds on ironies and will die of ironies in spite of the spur for life in members of Bivan's house. Who has ever eaten iron and survived?'

This was not going to be just another window-dressing show, Merima thought despairingly. He could see sparks in the mammoth crowd and they may start a fire that would consume him and the rest of the *knock-fists* as the UAC party apparatchiks called themselves. Who was it that said this rally should take place in Hamze a university town full of deranged professors out to place politicians on their promethean beds? The *knock-fists* were becoming knocked in the head to presume too much on the people's impotence. Well, well, well. He was on the podium already and must say something. Ordinarily he would have rehashed 'UAC' again to restore quiet, but the fear of another attack that may follow a shout of power from the crowd restrained him from giving the party's salute again. Instead, he began to speak as loud as the loudspeaker allowed.

'Things are getting better and they will continue getting better if you vote for UAC in the coming elections,' he began.

Most of the crowd cheered, some cheering without hearing what he had said. The essential character of Bivan's house was captured in these cheers. Those who heard Merima and cheered will most likely cheer him on in office whether he was performing or not. Those who did not hear him but cheered will most likely not be concerned with what he did with power when he got it.

Merima was encouraged by the response he had received and he plunged forward. 'We would improve water and power supply. Our farmers would have fertilizer at affordable prices. There would be free education from primary school way up to the university. A new sun is about to rise over Bivan's house that will be fair to everyone. Merima is that sun. A new moon that will never leave the sky plunging us into nights of darkness is about rising over Bivan's house. I am that moon.

'We have not started eating mud here as they are doing in other countries of the world,' he continued after a momentary pause during which he seemed to have been seized by a strange frenzy. We thank God we can still find food to eat. There is peace in Bivan's house. We thank God for the peace we enjoy. A little life is better than no life at all. In those countries of the world where the masses insist on change and better life than what they have, they are paying with their lives without assurance that their children would enjoy the better life they have sacrificed their lives for. Compromise is always better than insistence on getting all that you want. Even the government in England is a compromise - a mixed government of monarchy and democracy. That the government in England is a compromise has not made that country a less prospering nation than France whose government is not. The devil you know is always better than the angel you don't know. UAC!' he thundered again, climbing down the podium more hastily than he climbed up a while ago.

'Power!' the people roared.

On his seat up the dais opposite the podium, Merima watched the chairman and the organizing secretary of the party whispering into each other's' ears on the podium. Whatever they were saying must be very sinister. There was such a din of noise that if they talked like everyone was, no one was likely to hear them. That they were whispering in such noise meant what they were saying to each other was not a fair for those they were discussing. Merima was worried. He had expected after his speech the chairman of the party and the organizing secretary who were in charge of the rally would disband the rally, especially that there were signs of trouble, and everyone would go away. Even protocol demanded after the primehead candidate had spoken, the rally should wind up. But it seemed neither trouble nor protocol were being heeded by the chairman and the organizing secretary. The chairman of the party was a thug and it seemed there was nothing he liked more than brawls and skirmishes during political rallies. But did he even hear the parody of the party's power slogan given the noise in the square? Although the chairman had little education, he had a lot of exposure and was blessed with a keen native intelligence. So he was likely to understand the parody made in sophisticated English if he heard it. Like the chairman, the organizing secretary had little education. But many years of interaction with the English language had settled some measure of mastery of the language in him. So like the chairman he was likely to understand the derision of their party slogan.

'UAC!' Merima heard the chairman thundering into the loudspeaker.

'Power!' the crowd bellowed.

'UAC!' the chairman again cried into the loudspeaker.

'Sharing money equally!' majority of the people chorused. The voices of the few people who screamed 'power' were drowned by the voices of those who yelled 'sharing money equally.'

The chairman laughed. This was the kind of thing that tickled him. 'UAC; sharing money equally,' he drooled into the microphone. 'What can be fairer than that? Sharing money equally!'

'But the only thing that is shared here equally is the blistering heat,' an elderly man cried, interrupting the chairman.

The chairman uncharacteristically remained quiet while the elderly man inveighed him and his ruling party.

'Even the sun is not so equally shared,' the man continued. 'You are on the podium shielded from the sun by a tarpaulin and other big men like you are on the dais shielded from the sun by tarpaulins. As for money, if it is shared equally, it must be somewhere behind the curtain of misery hanging before us in this expansive square.'

'I believe the man that has spoken is a professor,' said the chairman, half statement, half question.

'And what if he is?' asked the elderly man.

The chairman was not a man of smooth manners, but a rough hand. He seemed to acquire a new panache as he was being assailed by the elderly man. 'With whom do you share your professorial chair?' he thundered at the elderly man.

'What is he saying?'

'You heard me. Professors elsewhere sit on their chairs only for a while and leave them for others; not here. You hold your title forever without sharing it with anyone and here you are making a caricature of politicians sharing money equally amongst themselves.'

'A professor's chair is earned. You are stealing public money and sharing it among crooks like yourselves.'

'Earned,' the chairman rejoined, sarcastically. 'Earned in a country no professor has ever been taken to the maternity under the labor of trying to give birth to an idea? At a time our campuses are swarming with twenty-for-a-penny professors? Ah!' he exhaled a stream of hot air from his nostrils. 'Earned ... who said earned things are not to be shared? The sweetest things to share to my mind are things that are earned.'

'Ah, Mr. Professor!' cried the organizing secretary now looking like an organized violence. 'Why don't you want to give up your chair for others standing to sit on? Why are you insisting on carrying it with you to the grave? Because everyone is sitting tight, every other person is standing loose. Why is everyone feeling naked here? Even when we had those leaves on, we weren't feeling this naked. The lawyer here is both solicitor and advocate. Elsewhere he is either advocate or solicitor. Why are we always trying to grab everything?'

'Your rotund cheeks chicken fed with our money are making you very cheeky,' said the elderly man.

'In the campus, you have chicks; why do you want to deny us our cheeks here? Keep your chicks and let us keep our cheeks,' said the organizing secretary, marching up to the elderly man with the ease of a thug to whom violence was a sport.

The elderly man stood where he was watching the organizing secretary walked to him sensing in the physics of his walk violence itching for release. Yet, the man could not will himself to move away from the approaching menace.

When the organizing secretary got to the elderly man, his huge hands swallowed up the neck of the elderly man in a vice grip, lifted him off the ground before setting him down again. 'They said you are a professor,' he breathed beer into the face of the elderly man, 'can you write on water?'

The elderly man now having multiple visions could not say anything. His face looked glazed and his breath was coming out in shallow gasps.

The chairman still standing on the podium was crying into the microphone, 'Kill him! Kill the swine! Kill all the professors! What's their use anyway?' He was stamping his right foot on the podium as he whirled round, microphone in hand shouting, 'kill the rebellious swine!'

Someone appeared from behind the organizing secretary and hit him with a bottle on the head. The secretary let go of the elderly man and turned to engage his assailant. Thugs of UAC and of the opposition Peoples Liberation Movement, engaged each other in fierce fisticuffs.

The chairman on the podium grinned wolfishly to himself. This was the sort of thing that made politics a worthwhile engagement and a game he would always love. Further away from the chairman, Merima was shaking his head as he was being led out of the square by his security aides.

Like Jamimi, Merima while in school was not interested in politics. Like Jamimi, Merima was a very studious student who held a lot of promise for scholarship. But, unlike Jamimi whose friends thought would be a good politician and persuaded him to join politics, Merima's friends said he was too soft for the game. But as soon as Merima left school, he joined politics because it was only from politics, he would be able to secure the material comfort he longed for. When he succeeds in politics, he would return to intellectual pursuits that his heart inclined him. When he decided to contest for political office, most of his supporters wanted him to contest for the office of common calabash. They said as a common calabash he was going to be nearer the people and so would be able to build his political future from the grassroots. But he knew the real reason for his supporters wanting him to become a common calabash was that they would be able to feast on him more. As a common calabash, if a man's child was sick, he came to him for financial assistance. If a man's family had nothing to eat, probably because the man had not worked hard enough to provide for his family, he went to the common calabash. If a man's pregnant wife went into labor and had to be taken to hospital, the man went to the common calabash for money to take her to the maternity. Sometimes the laboring wife was taken to the common calabash to excite such sympathy that would draw more money from him. This was usually the case if before the labor of the wife too many favors had already been sought from the common calabash.

Merima knew all these and it was part of the reason he did not want to contest for the office of common calabash. He had always wanted to be an archer and so he contested for the house of archery in his state. Being popular with the electorates, he won without much difficulty. Even as an archer he was frightened by the flood of demands for financial assistance that flowed to him. The more he tried meeting these demands, the more they came at him like an army of bees on the trail of a perfume. At a point, he was hiding from people waiting in front of his house or in his office to make demands on him. No single person coming to seek assistance from him had asked for a project that would benefit his community. It was always for the benefit of the person seeking the assistance.

After six years in the house of archery in his state, he contested for the house of archery of Bivan's house and was again elected; but this time more by rigging than by his popularity with the electorates. He had almost lost all his popularity with the electorates while in the state house of archery because he was not passing the elephant around for his supporters to cut the way they wanted. They said he was stingy and so they would no longer vote for him.

A big feast of one of the states knowing the mindset of the people, upon receiving the monthly allocation for his state from the central government had in a state-wide radio broadcast informed the people of the arrival of the allocation and asked them whether to share the money among them or use it to provide social services to them. Was the preference of the people not what democracy all about? the big feast had reasoned before making the broadcast. The big feast knew the reply he would get before he asked his question. The people preferred the money shared to them. Some of them even lauded him as being truly a big feast to provide occasion for such a big feast.

'Everything in politics and indeed outside politics in this country is about sharing and yet the sharing never seems to get round to everyone,' Merima complained one day to a fellow state archer when he was still in the house of archery.

'Probably because we are sharing the wrong things,' said the archer. 'You can never share money and it will reach everyone. But you can share a road among all the people of a state. In fact, the whole country can share a road. Until our people settle for that kind of sharing wealth, politics here will always be deceitful and dehumanizing.'

Because he could not share money to the people the way they wanted, he became unpopular with majority of those who thought he would be their meal ticket when he got to the house. When he contested for the central house of archery, he had to rely more on the rigging clout of his party than on his clout of popular support. In particular he had to rely on the support of Kamalun a powerful political godfather from his state. Like most high-profile politicians of Bivan's house, Kamalun was a political thug who fought his way up the political ladder by violence, subterfuge and treachery. How he got to the top of politics was how he remained there. Even by Bivan's house standards, he was so ugly in appearance and unrefined in manners and climate that he could not contest election himself and hope to *win*. But he was always in a position to sponsor a candidate with some respectability to win. Depending on his reading of a candidate he was sponsoring, he might dictate his terms of support before the election or after. His reading of Merima was that his terms of support would be unfolded after the election. Three months after the election, Kamalun called Merima one day to his massive house in Bodiga and told him what he expected from him as returns for his investments in him. From that month onward, Merima was to be making a monthly payment of 500,000 baduns into Kamalun's account for the remaining of his term in the central house of archery. In addition, he was to marry Kamalun's daughter who he had problems finding a husband for, because instead of resembling her mother who was a paragon of beauty, she resembled Kamalun who had no shred of physical appeal nor moral charm. The first and only time Kamalun contested for public office, it was a big headache for his campaign managers finding a public-charming photograph to use for his posters. In the morning, a photographer snapped Kamalun, but the picture was so ugly that nothing could be made of it. The managers thinking an afternoon picture would produce a better-looking Kamalun, told the photographer to come back in the afternoon for another picture. After all, even handsome people are not so handsome in the morning. In the afternoon another picture was taken, but it did not turn out any better. Another photograph in the evening did not produce a better picture either. There being nothing else they could do, his campaign organization had to make do with the pictures available to them. It was rumored he lost that election, particularly among women voters, because of his unseemly appearance. People close to him say part of the reason Kamalun did not want to contest election again was the impossibility of finding an appealing photograph for his posters.

For a while Merima said nothing. Creases on his forehead and twitches on his whole face showed he was thinking deeply about what he had just been told. Kamalun sat back on his chair, his small, sneaky eyes picking the face of his thinking political godson and probably future son-in-law.

After what looked to Kamalun like eternity, Merima looked him in the face and said he agreed to his terms. From what he had seen of Bivan's house's politics in recent times, Merima believed for a long time to come it was going to be a game in which victory would always lie with the contestant backed by the most formidable godfather. The people for a long time were going to have little influence in determining who their leaders would be having by their petty, individual demands sidelined themselves. Before election, the people wanted to be given something by political office seekers. A bar of soap, a measure of salt; other odds and ends were always shuffled around people's houses by politicians seeking their votes. The political godfathers supplied the money with which these items were purchased. On election day, voters again wanted to be given some cash before they would cast their votes for the candidates seeking them. The godfather supplied the money with which the electorates were settled. If thugs were needed, and they were always needed, the godfather supplied the attack-dogs. It was becoming inconceivable to think of getting elected or even appointed into a political office at whatever level of governance without the support of a political godfather. Merima liked Kamalun's style of making his demands after the election. He would accept his demands now so that he would have his support again when he makes a bid for the upper house of archery after which he would not contest for a political office again. After he was elected into the upper house of archery, he would refuse to accept any harsh demands his godfather would make on him and there was nothing he could do. Now he said yes to Kamalun's demands. Kamalun was happy and unknown to Merima, he began working underground for his political godson and son-in-law to clinch the primehead ticket of the United Action Congress in the next rounds of general elections. That was how Merima emerged as the primehead flagbearer of the UAC - the party that for more than thirty years had dominated the politics of Bivan's house.

Two weeks after his emergence as the primehead candidate of the UAC in the party's primary election, Merima was yet to come to terms with the fact that he was indeed the party's primehead flagbearer. How could a man that only wanted to be an archer end up as the primehead candidate of a vast country like Bivan's house and of a behemoth political party like UAC which was almost certain to *win* the election?

Unlike Jamimi, Merima was not a politician that stirred extreme emotions in the people. Standing alone without the support of Boyama the UAC primehead he would replace if he was declared winner of the election, most people were indifferent to him. But standing in the shadow of Boyama – a man said to be allergic to good reputation, a primehead despised by the people, the fire of the people's hatred for his patron blazed upon him.

Chapter Four

The political rally in Hamze was the third in the long campaign itinerary drawn up by the UAC primehead campaign council. Though little voting took place during elections in Bivan's house, UAC which always rigged elections insisted on campaigns - a shrewd tactic to invest a charade with legitimacy. Democracy and politics as measures of civilization must carry all the appearances they are known elsewhere even if in Bivan's house they were not honored with the morals or substance that made them true measures of civilization elsewhere. Vigorous campaigns by the UAC were part of the party's ploys of rigging election. If the party out-campaigned other parties, a landslide victory at the polls would be seen as the output of input. This election year, the need for vigorous campaigns was felt more than it had ever been because of the nomination of Jamimi as the primehead candidate of the Peoples Liberation Movement. Given Jamimi's popularity with the electorates, it would be more difficult than ever for the UAC to rig this election. So the party had to intensify its campaigns to generate an adequate smokescreen for rigging.

From Hamze, the UAC campaign convoy headed for Ogumta the former capital city of eastern Bivan's house. The road was full of potholes and bumps. By the railway level-crossing near Ogumta, the UAC convoy was brought to a halt by the campaign train of the Peoples Liberation Movement.

In an independent television network, the chairman of UAC had watched with amazement and fear the huge stir the PLM campaign train had caused in Bangora. He had immediately called Merima the primehead candidate of his party to lament what he had seen and believed Merima had.

'You know when I first heard of their intention to campaign by train, I never thought it would have this kind of effect on our people,' said the chairman in a bitter tone.

'I also didn't give it much chance of the success it is now having,' said Merima.

'Nothing beats a good idea,' said the chairman. 'With a sound idea, a man does not have to worry for his bread.'

'That's very true,' said Merima. 'But you know a brainwave is not something that comes to all people at the same time.'

'How I wish we first thought of this idea,' the chairman said, bitterly.

'I heard that this good idea came from the leader of the PLM,' said Merima in a voice that sounded mocking to the chairman.

'That was what you heard,' said the chairman in a contemptuous voice. 'I heard a different thing. What I heard was that the PLM primehead candidate gave his party this idea and even provided the money for the renovation of the train.'

'I am not surprised that was what you heard,' said Merima. 'You can never be trusted to hear and remember anything that is your failing.'

'What!' cried the chairman. 'A political upstart like you whom I am still wondering whether he deserves the huge privilege we have conferred on him speaking to me like this. Very soon you will regret what you have just said to me.'

'I don't think we should be screaming and threatening each other like this,' said Merima. 'Instead of threatening each other, we should be thinking of a way of taking the wind out of the sails of our adversary.'

'You started the stone-throwing,' said the chairman. 'When a man throws stones at me, I throw boulders at him. If you throw an arrow at me, I throw a spear at you. But now that you are sounding penitent, we will think of a way of hitting back at those spring chickens.'

After the little quarrel nothing more was said about the crowds the PLM train was pulling from village to village and from town to town until now that the UAC campaign convoy was forced to wait by the railway level-crossing till the PLM campaign train moved past. Inside, the train was packed full of PLM supporters, some hanging by the open doors of the train. On top of the train were countless people dancing and screaming, 'Bivan's house is for Jamimi, else...! UAC - thieves, rogues, bastards! Even before seeing the UAC campaign convoy, the PLM supporters had worked themselves into a frenzy of hate and contempt for the ruling party. On seeing the UAC convoy, their hatred and anger turned into a riot. Fortunately, the train was moving and so they could not attack the UAC convoy with their fists. Neither could the UAC supporters get on the train for a fight. But PLM supporters with sachets of water and other petty missiles threw them at the UAC convoy hurling insults at those they called a band of looters and barbarians let loose on the nation.

'No one will say we have not been provoked,' said the UAC chairman, sitting beside Merima and gnashing his teeth.

'I don't know what can be more provocative. To be halted in your tracks like a dog till your halter walked past you with a swagger of contempt or to be sprayed with insults as if you were a cockroach being fumigated out of a room you have no right to sneak into,' said Merima.

'A mere opposition party suspending the campaign of the government in power! Ah… where have you ever heard that kind of thing happening except in Bivan's house?' lamented the chairman, gnashing his teeth. 'If we have to wait on them like a herd of monkeys by the railtrack, we will soon have to stand behind them as their *aide de camp*. One thing leads to another, you know. Giving way to them on the road, we may have to give way to them in Jonka Palace very soon. Ahh… Something bad is coming. No, something bad will soon happen!'

'You are making too much of what should be a passing displeasure,' said Merima. 'They have a right to the railtrack as we have to the road.'

'Except that the rail is smooth while the road is rough.'

'The road is part of the rough and tumble of politics; or should I say the rough and tumble of corruption.'

'Call it what you like, but whoever thought of this train idea certainly has a head that is still working. No amount of money would have brought out the people I see on top of this train and by the railtrack. No spin of genial oration would evoke the excitement I see on their faces.'

'Certainly, no money can achieve what we are seeing now.'

'An idea has done this magic. And the annoying thing is that it is an idea close by, yet we could not see it before them. All you need to pluck this idea from your head is to see a campaign train as a campaign train and not a convoy of cars and buses waddling on the road like wonky ducks.'

'True, it is not an idea one will have to go to the river in search of. But ideas close by are the most difficult to see. The nose is just under the eyes, but how often do the eyes see it?'

'Ideas close by are actually commonsense. Commonsense I have found to be most uncommon. Indeed, often people talk of commonsense where there is no sense at all.'

'That train they are riding is the product of an idea,' said the chairman, absentmindedly. 'Ideas are the hub of the world. To my nose, there is nothing as sweet as a good idea. PLM is lucky to have on its ticket a man of intellect like Jamimi.'

If the aroma of intellect is so taking to this ape sitting beside me, why is he not ready to be in the kitchen and suffer the heat that delivers intellect? Merima wondered. 'Where have the birds fled to?' he said, changing the topic. 'We have been driving from Hamze to Ogumta for the past three hours and I haven't seen a single bird in the air though I have been scanning the skies most of the way. Have the birds fled the country?'

What's the matter with this man? the chairman wondered, angrily. Are we sure we don't have a lunatic on our ticket? A trifle is being made of us; we are being trampled underfoot by PLM caterpillars and instead of squaring his mind on how to hit back, he is talking of birds fleeing the country. Fine, if PLM succeeds in getting power, he may also have to flee the country like the birds. Jamimi no doubt will probe everyone who had held any position of consequence in the country. Merima as member of the house of archery was the chairman of the house committee on aviation. Jamimi will like to know why the aviation industry finally collapsed during his chairmanship of the aviation committee. He would have to fly away like the planes or the birds that flew away and never returned. Out of humor with what Merima had said; hoping to return Merima's vexatious amusement to him, he said, 'it is birds PLM's rumbling train and supporters' racket are hurling out of the country now. When they assume power, Jamimi would hurl into jail anyone who stole public money one way or the other.'

'You have been in this business for long, longer than I can conceivably remain in it.' said Merima, ignoring the insinuation in the chairman's statement. 'There is no vain animal like a politician. Nothing pains him like being ignored. There is nothing he gloats over like attention, like being the center of gravity around which everything revolves without being the center of responsibility from which performance flow. We can ignore PLM out of politics if we want.'

'Ignore them out of politics. That's fresh and exciting to me,' said the chairman. 'Before they rush us out of power, we will ignore them out of politics. That is pulsing to my heart and gripping to my mind.'

It took quite some time before the PLM long train pulled past the railway level-crossing to allow the UAC campaign convoy move on. It seemed to the UAC convoy that on seeing their convoy, PLM had deliberately slowed down the train to annoy them. From running on its feet, the train began to crawl on its knees.

'This is like a siege to me,' said Merima.

'If it is, the army laying it will die before us,' said the chairman. 'Any child that says his mother will not sleep, will also not sleep.'

After the last coach of the PLM train had crawled through the level-crossing, the UAC convoy began to move again, Merima fuming and swearing, the chairman looking sourly out of his car window. They arrived Ogumta towards sunset and began going through the streets of the town to mobilize support before going to the rally ground. They were booed and jeered at on Loguma street the first street they took. On the second street, they were not only booed and jeered at, they were pelted with stones. The first and second stone flew close to Boyama standing out through a jeep's sunroof. The third stone flew close to Merima's head also standing out through a jeep's sunroof. It missed him only by whiskers.

The chairman had different attitudes towards fisticuffs at political rallies and boos and jeers on the streets during political campaigns. While he did not mind fights during political rallies, he dreaded jeers and boos during street campaigns. From his experience, political rallies were mainly attended by political thugs and other mischief makers. The main object of such people attending political rallies was to foment trouble. For this reason, he was always unruffled by the boos and jeers of such fellows in a political rally. Not only was he not bothered, he was always ready to give to such miscreants what they were ready to give him. But people on the streets were different. They were in the main decent, non-violent folks who do not attack a political campaign moving through their streets out of mischief. If during campaign he was attacked by people on the street he was campaigning, he saw the attack as a true measure of his unpopularity. On such occasion, he was liable to be depressed and purged of all the fight in him. Now sitting behind Merima who was standing through the sunroof of the jeep, booed, jeered and stoned by the people along the street they were moving through, he felt wretched and advised Merima to sit down. But Merima wanting to show the chairman he was not all jelly as the chairman thought, would not sit down. 'There is only one God!' he said between locked teeth.

'And I haven't said there are two,' said the chairman. 'Discretion is the best form of valor.'

'I will not turn tail in this fight. We were beaten by the PLM at the railtrack and you want us to be beaten here as well? No way!'

'The sunroof is a place you acknowledge cheers, not jeers and stones,' said the chairman. 'Please, sit down.'

'No way. I …,' Merima began to speak again, but could not finish what he was trying to say before he was hit by a stone at the back of his head. He folded up on his seat inside the jeep.

'You see what I am telling you?' the chairman said. 'There are better ways of handling this sort of thing than the way you are. If that was a bomb or a grenade, your head would have been blown off. It would not have been funny continuing this campaign without your head on your neck.'

'You don't poke jokes over this sort of thing,' Merima fumed. 'But what is it of this people that Boyama ate during his tenure? The hatred is so thick that you can hang yourself on it.'

'They will not even wait for you to hang yourself on it. They will hang you on it.'

'I think we are risking too much having him on this campaign.'

'We may be risking far too much if we ask him to get off our back,' said the chairman. 'If he knows we resent him so much, he might decide to give power to PLM.'

'But that will be cutting his nose to spite his face.'

'From what I know of Boyama, he will drain his blood to spite his heart.'

'I think PLM left deposits of its poison here.'

'You are merely thinking, I saw the deposits of poison you speak about in the stones that were thrown at you. I only hope the stone that hit you didn't carry much poison into your blood stream.'

'If there is anything we don't lack in this campaign tumble, it is humor to laugh at ourselves.'

'Insults expect frowns. The best revenge on insult is a smile. In a way, a smile is an insult on insult.'

'There are days I think you wake up with wits playing drums in your head. I think today is one of those days.'

'Expecting cheers, we are receiving jeers,' said Merima in a depressed tone. 'Expecting boom, we are receiving boos; expecting whistles of adulation, we are receiving catcalls. It is so forlorn here.'

'We have seen how popular we are on the streets of this town. Let's go to the rally ground and see how popular we are there,' said the chairman. Without waiting for Merima's comment, he told the security aide sitting in front with the driver to radio the pilot car to speed up to the rally ground.

By the gate of the stadium where the rally would take place, the UAC campaign convoy saw a youth dressed like Merima - bearded, long-capped, horsetailed, warts and all. Tied round the youth's waist was a rope the loose end of which other youths were holding. One of the youths holding the rope was holding a whip which he was using to whip Merima's effigy, saying: 'Merima where is our money that you stole?'

The effigy cried out in pain, 'please, forgive me; I will bring it.'

The youths started chanting '*Merima mimi tido, Merima. Merima mimi tido,*' meant, 'Merima has stolen our money.' Other youths not far away from these youths were chanting, '*Mogo Bidi, mogonda; Mogo Bidi, mogonda. Si ko Jamimi, si ko Jamimi.*'

Mogo Bidi was the primehead candidate for the Democratic Peoples Alliance who had refused to join the grand coalition against the UAC by endorsing the candidacy of Jamimi. That was why PLM supporters were chanting he was a cow.

'PLM is really working,' said Merima as they drove into the stadium followed by jeers and curses of eternal damnation. Inside the stadium, Merima, the chairman and Boyama wasted no time in mounting the podium to address the rented crowd.

When Merima started talking, he raised his right hand with the victory sign made by his index and central fingers. 'The V-sign stands for VICTORY!' he bellowed, enthusiastically.

The crowd cheered, 'yes!'

'But it also means God and the people. In fact the V is made up of God and the people.'

The din that followed this declaration was louder than the first.

'Only that you have neither God nor the people!' someone cried in the silence that followed the din. 'God and the people stand for choice and consent not fraud and force which UAC stands for. UAC is the devil's experiment on earth of how his government will be in hell!'

'Damn the PLM supporters,' Merima swore under his breath. They have snatched from his lips what he wanted to say and turned it into a boomerang that has eaten deep into his belly. He wanted to say UAC has God and the people and so has victory only for the sons of Beelzebub to hit him below the belt. The same thing happened in Hamze. There was a hush after a din of approbation of UAC's salute and PLM used the hush to embarrass UAC. The thing onward was never to leave a hush their adversaries would use to snipe at them. But how could he be speaking without pausing? Damn PLM and its supporters. 'UAC has God and the people!' he continued putting on an expressionless face. 'Don't mind what the opposition has said. They lack manners. That's why they will never be given responsibility of leadership by the good people of this country.'

But as he was speaking he could see people leaving the stadium. He knew what was happening because it had happened before. The time the people were paid to come and be part of the rally had run out and they were walking away having done what they were paid to do. The delay they suffered arriving the stadium because of PLM's train has also caused this embarrassment. It was so galling. To pay rent on support can be very embarrassing indeed. It is a deal with a monkey that has no conscience. 'UAC!' he shouted.

It was largely the echo of his voice that came back to him. Most of the people were leaving and had no time to answer him.

Chapter Five

Every day after a campaign, Merima and eight members of the United Action Congress sat to review the day's campaign before retiring to bed. Initially Merima was not part of these post-mortems as the reviews were called; but later he saw the wisdom of being present. It was good for him to be present to know the contribution of each member of the campaign evaluation committee. From the contribution of the members, he would know who was intelligent, who was committed to the campaigns and those merely tagging along. Being part of the evaluation committee also helped him develop keener insights into the problems of the campaign and how to overcome them.

The campaign in Ogumta and UAC's level-crossing standoff generated a lot of heat in the post-mortem committee's meeting of that day. As always, Merima was the chairman of the meeting.

'We must find a way of avoiding the kind of embarrassment we suffered today in the hands of PLM from happening again,' said the party chairman. 'We are not pigs to be kept waiting beside a railtrack.'

'Well, you know Jamimi said we are dirty and ...' began a member of the committee.

'This is not a joking matter,' the party chairman snapped, looking grim.

'What are we to do?' asked a member of the committee, rhetorically.

'I think the best thing to do is to know PLM's campaign itinerary and avoid crossing paths with them in our campaigns,' said Makwu another member of the committee. He was a tall man with a far-away gaze that gave him a dreamy appearance.

If UAC still had a moral voice, Makwu might be said to be that voice. He was hardly on the same side of an issue with any of the party's apparatchiks largely because while they relied on fraud and force, he appealed to consent and choice. In the last general election which returned Boyama as the primehead of Bivan's house, there was a heated disagreement between Makwu and other party apparatchiks on whether the country's military should be used as security agents in the conduct of the elections. Boyama and the party chairman favored the use of the military. They said it was the best way to keep troubleshooters and mischief makers at bay. With the military prowling and growling around, every man of trouble and mischief would be held in check. This was what Bivan's house democracy, for its endurance and prosperity, required at this stage of its evolution,' the party chairman asserted with the air of an exponent of an indisputable truth.

'I agree with you that the military armed with their guns carry fear around with them in the nozzles of their guns and in the roll of their eyes; but I thought an election day, a day of franchise, is a day of freedom for the people,' said Makwu.

'I can see where you are going,' said Boyama.

'Fear and freedom do not sit on the same table, isn't it? Fear is water that puts out freedom, isn't it? Well, perhaps you are right. But let me tell you something. Democracy is not a drink you take in one gulp, no matter how much you like its taste. Like whisky you must take it in little sips, else you will not be able to handle the madness that will follow.'

'Your Excellency, what exactly do you mean?' asked Makwu.

'I mean what you hear,' said Boyama. 'How long have we lived with democracy? How do you surrender yourself completely to a whore you just picked on the street, however seductive, unless you are drunk? Democracy is still a whore with us. It is not yet our wife. It is not even yet our mistress.

'Someone called it the whore of the sovereign,' said a party elder present at the meeting.

'And I think it is not an inappropriate nickname,' said the party chairman. 'Come to think of it, every woman that has been prominent in politics in Bivan's house has had something to do with prostitution at some point of her life.'

'Whore of the sovereign!' someone exclaimed. 'It's no doubt an appropriate nickname, except that I don't know who is sovereign here.'

'Sovereign here is every individual person pooled into the unit called Bivan's house,' said Merima. 'But in England, sovereign is the monarch and the liaison of this whore with the monarch in England was what delivered the House of Lords. The hermaphrodite, I mean the mixed government of England came out of the consort between the whore of the sovereign and the sovereign.'

'What you are saying is very true,' said a member of the post-mortem committee. 'The government in England is a compromise between democracy and monarchy.'

'Someone said it is an enlightened fraud on democracy,' said another member.

'Elsewhere it is a compromise between anarchy and dictatorship,' said the chairman.

'Here it may end up as a castration of choice and consent by fraud and force,' said Makwu. 'When I was a child, I always shuddered when a pig was being castrated behind our house. The screams of the pig were so nerve-wracking. I go through the same nerve-wracking experience with our democracy.'

'Democracy is like the snake in the Garden of Eden,' said the chairman. 'There are many nations it has betrayed to sorrow and gnashing of teeth. You can't be too optimistic about it. But what I know is that democracy is a government of different variants. Our variant of democracy is freedom surrounded by fear. Freedom if you don't know can be a rascal. To prevent it from becoming a rascal, fear is needed. If you have any doubt of the potentials of freedom to breed rascality, the story of the prodigal son might remove such doubt. Finding himself surrounded by freedom without the fear of his father's rebuke, the prodigal son squandered all he had before he knew where he was.'

'I see fear making democracy a rascal here than freedom would have,' said Makwu. 'We are moved by fear to want to hold to power at all cost. Our fear propels us to use force on the electorates who, moved by fear that we will loot the nation, resist us.'

As far as Makwu was concerned, it was the involvement of the military in elections that always marred them with violence. Over the years, military coups had made the military partisans in politics and whenever they were drafted to supervise the conduct of election, they were often found to support one party or the other. The UAC in power used the largesse of office to bribe the military to support them during election. Before election, military officers were bought state-of-the-art cars by the government or given choice plots of land in different cities of Bivan's house. During election the bribed military was called in to rig the party back to power and then used force to crush any public protest against the fraudulent election. Thus, it came to pass that Bivan's house military were no longer capable of staging coups that install them in power, but coups against the people during election by rigging the election for the ruling party. The police were no better. There was a bizarre incidence of a man going to a police station to complain about election rigging in a polling station only to find the police thumb-printing for the UAC at their station.

Now irked by Makwu's suggestion that they study PLM's campaign itinerary so as to avoid being embarrassed as they were that day, the chairman full of pent-up anger said, 'Makwu, it is difficult to know why you are in UAC. As they say, if you can't stand the heat why not get out of the kitchen? What you are saying now is that we re-draw our campaign itinerary to suit the idiosyncrasies of the PLM such that if by our already drawn itinerary we are supposed to be in Wandugu tomorrow, but it turns out that PLM is also going to that town on the same day, we should take our campaign to another city or stay in our houses or hotel rooms till PLM has finished its campaign in Wandugu and left. How does that sound in your ears?'

'I won't put it exactly the way you are putting it,' said Makwu.

'How then would you put it, if you won't put it exactly the way I am putting it?' asked the chairman.

'I will say we can either arrive Wandugu earlier or later than them,' said Makwu.

'A little early or a little late, gives us the miss we are looking for, is that not it Makwu?' said another member of the committee.

'Let us not be playing politics with ourselves,' said Merima; 'scoring ourselves instead of the other team. Your suggestion Makwu as I understand it is that one day we will run as fast as the hare to avoid PLM and another day crawl like the tortoise to avoid meeting our opponents. I don't know the reputation of the hare and tortoise in the folk stories your grandmother told you. But in the folklore my own grandmother told me, the hare and the tortoise have very unsavory reputation. Already our reputation as a party has little to recommend us for public patronage; if we add to our bad reputation the unsavory reputation of the hare and tortoise, I think even our families would not stand our sight.'

'Who is the railway manager that leased the train to PLM?' asked the party chairman, his face squeezing into an ugly scowl.

'That train must have been leased to them by the railway corporation headquarters in Babudo,' said Merima.

'And it would not be without the authority of the corporation's Director-General,' a member of the post-mortem committee said.

'Why should he do such a thing?' asked another member of the committee, heatedly.

'Why should he not do such a thing?' asked Makwu. 'Trains are there for hire. They are either hired by the general public or a section of it.'

'Makwu, you might be right that trains are there for hire,' said the chairman. 'But when the hiring is for politics, prudence demands that the Director-General needs be more circumspect. I think he is tired of his job. At any rate, he is close to retirement. So, he may as well go. I only hope he made something for himself from the lease he granted the PLM on which he and his family would live, because I don't see him getting gratuity or pension for a long while to come, if ever.'

'Retiring the Director-General does not mean retiring the PLM campaign train from the railtracks,' said a member of the committee. 'We still have to stand at attention if not with a salute as the PLM train crawls past us with a swagger, if not contempt.'

'About that we shall see,' said the chairman. 'If PLM members see themselves as angels, what they don't know is that the devil is always ahead of angels in plots and schemes in situations like this.'

Chapter Six

Jamimi and his campaign train got to Aula station around 4p.m. According to the campaign itinerary, the campaign team was to disembark from the train in Aula station and travel to the populous upcountry town of Kollu by road. When they got to Aula, their vehicles had been stationed there for more than an hour waiting for their arrival.

The journey from Aula to Kollu was a two-hour journey, but it took Jamimi and his campaign team more than five hours. At different points of the road, villagers who knew the PLM primehead campaign team would go through that road that day kept bringing the campaign convoy to a halt. Even in forested parts of the road, people sprung up from nowhere waving sheaves of corn – the PLM symbol and chanting anti-UAC slogans. In these lonely spots of the road where there were these sporadic and sudden appearances of ecstatic bands of supporters on the road, it seemed to Jamimi as if forest spirits and not people were rising up to cheer them on. He shared his thoughts with Talgon sitting next to him.

'So, it seems to me also,' said Talgon, looking fascinated. 'I believe the spirits of our ancestors long dead have joined the struggle to rid our dear nation of the UAC scourge. 'I can even see headhunters long dead who started politics in Bivan's house siding with us in this epic struggle.'

'Even without us pouring libation of gin to rally them to our support?' asked Mengo the secretary of the party, an amused expression on his face. He was a man with a hung face and a little jowl that raised him to an age he was yet to attain. He was always wincing like a man that had swallowed a bee that was stinging him inside his stomach.

'The tears of the poor of this raped country are enough libation of gin,' said Talgon.

'Talking about rape reminds me of a joke someone made concerning the naming of a recreational resort in Pambe by Boyama as virgin resort,' said Jamimi.

'What was the joke?' Talgon asked. Another person would have gone ahead to tell the joke, but not Jamimi. He always waited to be baited and cajoled to pass a joke on or express his mind on what he considered a frivolous matter.

'He said how can a nation which has been serially raped by her leaders have a virgin resort?'

Talgon laughed. 'You know if self-ridicule were a scheme that develops a nation, Bivan's house would have been the most developed nation on earth. Remember the joke about Bivan's house Electricity Board that only serves to remind people of candles in the wind or the ancient days of flaring tapers moving from hut to hut in the deep dark night. Someone said hell is divided into countries the same way the earth is. Sinners in hell are not in a lake of fire, but tortured with electrical instruments which require electricity to function. All at once, it seemed at a point, every inmate of hell wanted a visa to Bivan's house part of hell. When the reason for this sudden preference for Bivan's house's hell was investigated by the devil, it was found that there was little or no torture going on in Bivan's house's hell because there was always power outage and so the torture instruments rarely had power to function.'

In a small town about fifty-eight kilometers away from Kollu, the PLM campaign convoy found women wrappers spread on the road as mats of honor for the

PLM convoy to ride over. This touching act of support moved Jamimi to tears.

'The volume of support we receive from the poor of this country is proportionate to the volume of suffering the people go through under the UAC misrule,' said Jamimi.

'I agree,' said Talgon. 'I believe there is no nation on earth that has ever been subjected to the misrule this nation has gone through in the last eleven years. Yet, last year when there was a protest in Ekwedo state, Boyama wondered why. More like the devil wondering what is wrong with hell.'

'In the history of this nation, there is no politician that has ever excited the support of poor people like you,' said Mengo to Jamimi.

'True and this is because things have never been so bad as under UAC. Look at the termite and locusts' action they are taking on our money.'

'The burden of performance cast on you if we win this election, which we will damn well win is therefore heavier than any ever cast on a politician,' said Talgon.

This is life thought Jamimi. In life, there is never an excess of benefit over burden. One way or the other everything must be paid for and often, you pay in excess of the value of things you receive. He was sought after because of a benefit the people believed he would bring to them and to give the people the benefit they hoped for will entail no little burden for him. The benefit of support being given to him now is a burden in the shawl of benefit.

'Life is walking away from us and we seem short of voice to call it back,' he heard Talgon saying. 'Diamonds are selling at 50 dollars per carat, but the value of the poor man's life in this country is less than 1 dollar per soul. The per capita misery in this country keeps burgeoning as the per capita income keeps shrinking.'

'Nature hates a vacuum,' said Mengo. 'If wealth is shrinking in the country, poverty will occupy the space left by the departing wealth. It is a world of *his place let another take.* When one thing leaves, another succeeds it. By whatever means, spaces must be occupied.'

'But, Talgon and Mengo, how can you be talking of a shrinking per capita income and a burgeoning per capita misery for everyone when people in government are getting richer every day?' asked Jamimi.

'This is the problem with per capita income,' said Talgon. 'Money is fictionally shared equally to everyone by socialism, but practically shared to only a few by capitalism. There is nothing as pleasant as the quixotic concept of per capita income to the thieving government official. He steals and eats alone the money that has already been shared equally to everyone by per capita income.'

'The fingers are not equal; therefore, when you dip them into the soup, they will not carry equal amount of soup,' said Mengo.

'You have said something there,' said Jamimi.

'Talgon, does this not prove to you that socialism may succeed in theory, but it is capitalism that will carry the day in practice?' asked Mengo, a look of mischief on his face.

'If it were only carrying the day, things might not be this bad. But it is also carrying the night, a deep dark night,' said Jamimi, a doleful look on his face.

'Even in theory, socialism has already ceded the levers to capitalism. Why per capita and not per socia?' said Mengo. 'Whoever came up with per capita income is a thief.'

'Even in the face of the gross inequality in wealth distribution, I still maintain that every man's per capita income is shrinking while the per capita misery is burgeoning,' said Talgon with the spark of an insight on his face. 'Per capita should not be seen in terms of material possessions only. Security is also a species of per capita income. When material wealth shrinks for the poor, security shrinks for the rich. A wise man once said, 'the poor cannot sleep because they are hungry; the rich also cannot sleep because they know the poor are awake.' *The child that says his mother will not sleep will also not sleep.'*

'It is only ants that do not sleep and remain fine,' said Mengo.

'Even the dolphin that is so concerned with its security must sleep, though it sleeps with one eye open,' said Jamimi.

At the outskirts of Kollu, mats were spread on the road for Jamimi and his campaign team to ride over. It was dusk. The mass of people united with the darkness of the night rolled into a solid band of darkness with little hues of light.

'The sun is out. Even the leprous hand of UAC cannot cover it,' said a man holding a loudspeaker. 'The anger of the people is barking and the night marauder has nowhere to run to. The hunger of the poor man has delivered a child that is asking those who stole the poor man's food "Where is my food?" The sun has risen. Where is the devil that has been strutting in the dark?'

Chapter Seven

Of all states in Bivan's house, Hatto state stood out as the state where politics was based on issues and not sentiments of tribe and religion. Damish a local politician spent almost thirty years of his life to produce this situation in Hatto. Everywhere he went, he told the people that politics is a game of interest, not tribe and religion. 'If anyone brings tribe or religion into politics, he is doing so to advance his selfish interest and not that of the people. Elsewhere, election is an investment for the electorate, but service for the politician presenting himself for election. Here politicians seeking election see election as an investment for themselves and a duty for the electorates. The electorates must say NO to this. Election must be an investment for the electorates and service for the elected. A wise voter invests his vote in someone he has reasonable prospects of good returns from. Representative democracy has evolved because we cannot all participate in governance. We have to elect some of our number to run our affairs. To elect someone to represent you means you are asking him to go do for you what you would have done for yourself were you at the place you are sending him. If something is required to be said there, he will say for you what you would have said for yourself were you at the venue of representation. If anything is shared there, he should bring your share to you. Electing someone to represent you in a democracy is not different from the custom our forefathers evolved of sending one of their number to represent them in a wedding ceremony. We all know that custom and I believe we have all been beneficiaries of it. If there is a wedding ceremony in a faraway village, a member of the clan is sent to the wedding ceremony to represent the clan because the whole clan cannot go to the wedding. The representative sent by the clan would speak not for himself at the wedding, but for the whole clan. If he is given meat and other victuals of ceremony, he does not eat these things alone at the wedding ceremony or branch into the bush on his way home to eat them alone. He brings them home and they are shared among members of the clan. It is the same thing with democracy. Those you elect must be people you trust. Only that in a democracy those you are to elect need not be from your clan, tribe or religion, at least in the traditional way we know tribe, clan and religion. I am saying in the traditional way we know clan, tribe and religion because I can see new clans, tribes and religions that have nothing to do with the clans, tribes and religions that we know emerging. The clans, tribes and religions we know before now have blood and God as the ties that bind them together. But the new clans, tribes and religions emerging have money and wealth as the tie binding them together. This tie I have found to be stronger in today's world than the ties of blood and God. Like I always tell you, if blood is thicker than water, interest is thicker than blood. Today, there are only two clans: the clan of the rich and the clan of the poor; only two tribes: the tribe of the rich and the tribe of the poor; only two religions: the religion of the rich and the religion of the poor. This is how matters currently stand and do not allow anyone in the pursuit of his own selfish interest deceive you to the contrary. Economic tribes are what are important today; not linguistic tribes. The government is one tribe. The governed is another tribe. Emerging tribal wars should be fought between these new tribes. This crave for chiefdoms, this clamor for more states we see everywhere is not unconnected with the desire of people that power be their tribesman, speaking their own language. But the only way power can be your tribesman is for you to be able to control it and you can only control it if you own it. You can only own it if you generate it.

'The problem of Bivan's house is that the poor weren't involved in the struggle for independence. In Holga, the Bambo involved ordinary Holgans in the struggle for independence and that is why they are involved in the fight against oppression after independence. Holgans fighting oppression now are children of the Bambo fighters of old. As their parents were involved in the fight to free Holga from colonial oppression, they are involved in the fight to free Holga from the oppression of local elites after independence. As the parents of the poor of this country weren't involved in the struggle for independence, their children are not involved in the current struggle against oppression. The poor of this country have always been onlookers of the politics and economics of the nation.'

Damish went to prison several times for asking people to insist on their rights and demand for justice, but he stuck to what he believed in to his death. Basoi the primehead of Bivan's house then was suspected to have a hand in his death. Damish had in a political rally called on Bivan's house members to insist on justice. The following day the ceremonial feast for internal affairs accused Damish of inciting people to rebellion and said he could be charged to court for sedition. When Damish read the accusation of the ceremonial feast, he organized another rally in which he said, 'This is both ridiculous and interesting. How can my telling people to insist on their rights and justice amount to inciting them to rebellion? What is the government of Basoi telling the people? Is it saying it is an unjust government that denies people their rights? If not, why should it be uncomfortable and jittery over a mere advice to the people to insist on their rights and justice? Members of Bivan's house you may judge for yourselves.'

Two days after this rally, Damish died. Gawuro his friend said he was poisoned by the man he regularly bought cigarette from. According to Gawuro, Damish was killed by Basoi because he had gone beyond inciting people by his radical exhortations to ridiculing the government which is the worse form of incitement.   Gawuro   claimed   a cigarette seller was bribed with a lot of money to insert *tebi* into Damish cigarette. The cigarette seller whose children were out of school because he could not pay their school fees and who could hardly feed his family said to himself, 'What is my own in politicians' fight? What is my own if they agree? If they fight, I suffer. If they agree, I still suffer. As they say, when two elephants fight, the grass suffers. But the grass still suffers when two elephants make love. Of what use is any of them to my life or that of my children? They pitch the poor against each other, then exploit their fight to make money. Why can't the poor exploit their fight to make money also?' He accepted the money and did as he was told.

Damish was dead. But he had lighted candles in the heads of people before he died. Winds of deception came, but the candles lit by Damish kept burning like electric bulbs in a tunnel. In Bivan's house it was said there were two ways a national or provincial politician could get political support in a locality. He could get it directly from the people or through local heavy weight politicians who the people respected. In

Hatto, there was only one way such a politician could get the support of the people: directly from the people themselves.

UAC always dreaded campaign in Hatto state because in this state, deception sold in other parts of Bivan's house could not be sold. There was a saying in Hatto that it is issues that buy votes in Hatto, not sentiments of tribe or religion. Face up the issues, face down the sentiments were popular electorates' slogans in Hatto.

Because of its lack of support in Hatto state, whenever UAC was going on a primehead campaign in Hatto town, it sneaked into the town, days ahead of the campaign, mercenary supporters called 404s - political dogs. This way it diluted the antagonism it would receive to such an extent that support and opposition interplayed to give the party a balance sheet that said it stood a chance of winning an election in Hatto as any other party - support and opposition being nearly balanced. This kind of impression in Hatto which was the barometer of issues-driven politics and political morality was an open sesame for the UAC. With such an impression, it could rig election in the whole country and say that even in Hatto it was supported during the campaigns leading up to the election.

From Ogumpta, the UAC primehead campaign convoy swept into Hatto expecting to be received by its armies of mercenary supporters. But this year PLM supporters in Hatto were prepared for the UAC mercenaries and their host the Hatto chapter of the UAC. Most of the UAC mercenary supporters were camped in the UAC secretariat in Hatto. On the day the UAC primehead campaign entourage was coming to Hatto for campaign, PLM supporters after observing that the mercenaries and the Hatto UAC party executive members were in the secretariat preparing to go out and receive the primehead campaign team, locked up all exit points of the secretariat and surrounded the secretariat armed with machetes, cutlasses and petrol daring the mercenaries to attempt coming out. Even though the PLM supporters that surrounded the secretariat resented the mercenaries' coming to Hatto to give the UAC an appearance of support the party did not enjoy in Hatto, what they really wanted to achieve by the barricade was to prove to themselves that they could thwart UAC's rigging of election in collation centers after election. The barricade therefore was a dress-rehearsal of what they would do at various collation centers in Hatto in the coming election.

Unknown to the PLM supporters, the mercenaries were just too happy to be prevented from going out of the secretariat. They had no iota of love or support for the UAC. They were only mercenaries paid to cheer the UAC - a task some felt sick to perform, but accepted to because of the money. If therefore an opportunity not to perform like this offered itself, they were too glad to seize it. To the shock of the PLM supporters, the mercenaries they thought would give them a fight, gave no fight at all. The party executive members knowing they stood no chance daring the PLM supporters without the support of the mercenaries also gave no fight.

Merima and his campaign convoy were shocked to find no mercenary supporters or the party executive members on the outskirts or streets of Hatto. Usually, the mercenary supporters and the party executive members received the primehead campaign entourage at the outskirts of the town and together they drove to the secretariat of the party inside the town with the mercenaries chanting UAC *si ko mee du*! An annoying and sickening thought began to brew in the mind of the party chairman. The organizing secretary must have cornered the money he was given to pay the mercenaries and that was why there were no mercenaries on the streets. Before, mercenary fees were handed over to the party executive of any state where mercenary support was needed. But most of the state party executives to whom such money was given lined their pockets with the money instead of hiring mercenaries. Because of this, the national executive of the party had decided to saddle the national organizing secretary with the responsibility of hiring mercenaries. After all the primehead campaign was a national affair. But from the look of things, what the party sought to avoid by removing this responsibility from states party executives, it had found in the national organizing secretary. Each year fees for mercenary support kept rising because mercenaries kept complaining that their work was becoming dirtier and riskier each year as the UAC became more unpopular. It was as if each mercenary was seeing himself as a carat of diamonds whose price must go up every day.

This year, the party had had to cough out a hundred million baduns to pay mercenary supporters for the Hatto campaign alone. Some years back, this huge sum of money was a state's budget for a whole year. And this was the money the organizing secretary had ambushed and taken to his hole. But, what of the party executives in Hatto? If the mercenaries were not at the outskirts of the town and on the streets to receive them because they had not been paid, what of the party executives? Or were they now also mercenaries that must be paid? Exasperated, he turned on the organizing secretary wanting to know what he did with the money he was given to organize things in Hatto.

'I used it for what it was meant.'

'If that's true, why can't I see the money on the streets of Hatto. Our money used to hang on tree branches wherever we went. I have scanned the branches and I haven't seen any badun on a tree branch.'

'I tell you the money was used to hire 404s,' said the organizing secretary unable to meet the chairman's steady and probing stare. He had used only half of the money on mercenaries and kept half for himself. That was what everyone in politics was doing, particularly at election time like this. It was an unwritten rule of politics, but a rule known to everyone: campaign and election money were not accounted for. That being the case, whenever money strayed into one's hand for one thing or the other, it would be foolish not to put something by for oneself, especially in a system that was loyal to no one. When the system eventually betrays you to the dogs of irrelevance, it was what you put by your side that would come to your aid. Could it be because he did not give the mercenaries the whole money that they were not on the streets? he agonized. But they did not know how much he was given, or has his enemies in the party betrayed him to the dogs? The mercenaries actually demanded for only seventy million baduns. He was the one that jacked up the money to a hundred million baduns believing no one would find out how much the mercenaries asked for. Hiring mercenaries wasn't something anyone in the party wanted to talk about and no one looked too closely at the deals that eventually brought on the mercenaries. When he was given the hundred million baduns he asked for, he felt he should be able to make fifty million from the transaction and so instead of paying the mercenaries seventy million, he paid them fifty. Now the mercenaries were nowhere to be seen thereby blowing the lid off his scam. He was feeling feverish even though the weather was hot. The cold eyes of the chairman on him might by literary conjecture be thought to create this effect on him. But it was not only the mercenaries that were not at the outskirts of the town and on the streets. Even the Hatto UAC party executive members were not in these places. If he was blamed for the absence of mercenaries, he couldn't be blamed for the absence of the party executives.

'But even the party executives are nowhere to be seen,' said the organizing secretary. 'I can't be blamed for their absence also.'

'Mercenaries provide cover for them,' said the chairman. 'If mercenaries refused to come out, the party executive members may feel too naked coming out alone in this unfriendly territory.'

'I don't believe that our party has become so unpopular as to make even local chapters of the party seek the protection of mercenaries before coming out to receive a primehead campaign team,' said the organizing secretary, tremors dotting his voice.

'If local chapters do not need the services of mercenaries, why do they employ them for their big feast and other campaigns?' asked the chairman.

'I rather think there is some mischief playing itself out in this town which is responsible for what we are seeing,' said the organizing secretary, trying to control his rising panic.

'Or some mischief had already played itself out when someone decided to appropriate money meant for a particular task,' said the chairman.

'Chairman, believe me, I paid the mercenaries what I was given to pay them.'

'Then why are they not on the streets?'

'Mercenaries are mercenaries,' said the organizing secretary. 'They are the most unreliable beings on earth. Anyone who can support you for money can't be stable in character. They are as unfixed as a fluff of cotton in the wind. If you can buy a mercenary to support you, he can be bought at a higher price not to support you.'

'Cut out that crap,' the chairman said unable to contain his rising irritation. 'Who is that person in Bivan's house with a higher price than UAC? As for mercenaries being unreliable beings, who in this life is not a mercenary? Apart from musicians, who, but for the money he is paid, enjoys what he is doing? We are all mercenaries doing what we are doing for money. Period! We are all sieged into mercenary behavior by the wolves of necessities which are increasing every day. Since we are all mercenaries, does it follow by your thesis that we are all unreliable? I don't think so. We are only unreliable where there is no money or there is short of it. But where there is money, we all, or at least most of us, recognize our duty to do what we are paid to do. If you have bitten off part of the money or in fact carted the whole of it to your hole, as it now appears to me, say so and stop trying to pull wool over the eyes of a bat that can see in the dark.'

'I swear, I gave them the money,' the organizing secretary said without conviction in his voice.

'The empty streets are saying you didn't.'

'Chairman, I swear I did.'

'What are you swearing by?' asked the chairman.

For a while the organizing secretary could not say anything. It was difficult to say why he could not find a reply to such a simple question.

'This is part of our problem,' said the chairman. 'We are running out of things to swear by to make others believe us. Before, it was God that was readily available to be sworn by. Now we have desecrated God by our actions and our utterances and nemesis are not forthcoming. So swearing by God no longer excites belief.   What we don't know is that other human beings have passed the way we are passing now - a way littered with broken values and broken meanings; a cannibalistic world in which men ate men. But in the end, they had to retrace their steps when it appeared anyone was fair game in the war of each against all. They began to organize society on values and meanings that secured each against all. This is the foundation of the civilization that we inherited. Eventually we will reach the precipice they reached and retrace our steps or perish.'

The organizing secretary did not say anything. In fact, he only half heard what the chairman had said. His mind was engrossed by the betrayal of the mercenaries. At least he gave them more than half of what they asked for. The chairman was talking of anyone being fair game in abstraction when in reality he was such a fair game that has just been shot down. Well, they cannot just collect fifty million baduns, feed fat on it and go to sleep on their beds without hearing from him. He certainly will go after them as he was sure the party will come after him, at least for a refund of the money.

'Since we left Ogumpta, I haven't seen much of our posters on the road either,' said the chairman. 'I hope like mercenaries they had not fled the trees and electric poles they were posted.'

'I believe PLM supporters had removed our posters posted along the way from Ogumpta to Hatto. The publicity secretary told me he personally supervised the posting of the posters,' said the organizing secretary, more at ease now that accusations had shifted from him to the publicity secretary.

'Where were the posters posted?'

'The publicity secretary said on tree stems and milestones along the road.'

'That's wrong,' said the chairman. 'Our posters can only remain where you posted them if posted on tree branches high up where they cannot easily be removed.'

'But, chairman, it is increasingly becoming difficult for us to operate. Apart from hiring mercenary supporters, we have to hire palm wine tappers to climb tall trees and paste posters for us since we cannot climb the trees to do so.'

The chairman felt like laughing, but suppressed the urge because laughing would lighten the torment on the organizing secretary's conscience, which he observed had already been lightened by the shift of concern from the absence of mercenaries to the absence of posters.

'But chairman,' said the organizing secretary when the chairman lapsed into a silence he found oppressive. 'If you observe, there are very few people on the streets. It is not just a matter of mercenaries and our party executive members being not on the streets; it seems even the PLM supporters who literally own the town are nowhere in the town. I think something bad must have happened. The people are either dead or have fled the town.'

The chairman had also observed a particular desolation in the town, but did not want to raise it lest he made things easy for the organizing secretary. But now that he had raised the matter, he said, 'I have also observed that the town is near desolate. I wonder what all these means.'

'I am beginning to inhale something sinister in the air,' said the organizing secretary.

I will rather say you are beginning to breathe easier, thought the chairman.

When the chairman did not say anything, the secretary continued, 'Well, whatever it is, I believe at the party secretariat we will find out.'

No one spoke again until they got near the party secretariat. As they moved near the secretariat, the noise of people in the secretariat began to tell them why the town was almost empty. When they turned a corner that delivered the secretariat to their view, what they saw shocked them. The whole town seemed to have gathered at the party secretariat for what they were yet to know and did not move close enough to know. The gesticulations they saw where they were and the weapons they saw being waved in the air told them they would not be received with hugs and handshakes, but with hacks and slashes. Immediately they made a U-turn and headed back the way they came pursued by jeers and curses.

Chapter Eight

'Your Excellency, how is the whore of the sovereign?' Merima's wife asked him after he returned from Hatto.

'So even our wives have latched up to the persuasion that politics is the whore of the sovereign?' said Merima a look of surprise on his face. 'To answer your question, when I left her in her brothel, she was in a fit of temper I could not stand. In fact, I fled home from her.'

'For the past seven days that you have been away on campaign, I have asked myself several times, apart from politics, what is it that can keep a man away from his family this long and the only answer that kept coming to me was a whore who men sometimes give the pleasant title of mistress to. Beer cannot do such a thing. No matter how drunk a man is, he staggers home late in the night to his family. But the whore or mistress would not let go without a fight. So there is no better name for politics than the whore of the sovereign.'

'No one will say this name does not wrap politics the way mud wraps up a pig,' said Merima. 'You know another meaning for *whore* is someone ready to set aside principles or personal integrity for selfish ends, and that's what politicians are. Again, someone said politics is an ass everyone can ride on. This also answers to the reputation of politics as a whore of some sort.'

'So how has it been with the whore of the sovereign or the ass?'

'So, so my dear,' Merima said, tonelessly.

'You look so, so yourself,' said the wife. 'What has been happening on the campaign tumble all the days you have been away?'

'The ass is getting more unruly every passing day. Look at my head,' said Merima, turning to show his wife where he was hit by the stone. The spot was still swollen.

'God!' the wife caught her breath in shock. 'Who did this to you?'

'The unruly ass of course! It booted me on the head.'

'Please, cut out the metaphors. Who did this to you?'

'The sad thing is that I don't know who did it. But it was in Ogumta.'

'Politics, the whore of the sovereign! Why is she more wayward and violent in Bivan's house? Indeed, why is everything here always more violent? Hunger is more violent, disease is more violent, the sun is more violent, ignorance is more violent; even love and laughter are more violent here; why? Your Excellency, what dealt this injury on your head, or as you don't know who did it, you don't know what did it?'

'A stone.'

'A stone? Like Delilah, the whore of the sovereign is seeking to destroy my husband. But I will not allow that. I invoke leprosy and paralysis on the hand that threw that stone. It is the last stone that hand that massage the whore of the sovereign will ever throw.'

'I never knew you were given the power to invoke curses.'

'When the life or prosperity of a husband is threatened, the destiny of his wife is threatened. And who is threatening the life of my husband? A whore and a witch I possess the material properties to be if I am moved by spite for the world to.'

'Should I then jump out of the river before the flood rises to my mouth now that my legs are only knee-deep?' Merima asked, a little astounded by his wife's outburst.

'Perhaps you should,' said the wife, lapsing into a thoughtful silence.

'Very well then,' said Merima with what looked like a gleeful expression on his face. 'Tomorrow I will tell my party I am no longer running. They should find a replacement for me.'

For a long time, the wife did not say anything. She was obviously in deep thought. 'Never!' she said at last. 'If you turn back, you will find a worse ass behind you. Like most people who went to school, I believe you have read about the mountain of wild fleece in Faukan country. In case you haven't, the mountain of wild fleece collected all the wealth of Faukan country to its top where the wealth grew wild without an owner because the owners had been left high and dry at the foot of the mountain and in far flung regions. Whoever was able to climb the high mountain was free to take as much wealth as he needed from the mountain. Because there was neither let nor hindrance in what a man could grab for himself at the top of the mountain, no one had ever climbed the mountain and came down of his own volition. Because there was very little wealth at the foot of the mountain and in far flung regions of Faukan country a climber of the mountain felt sieged by poverty at the foot of the mountain and so was unwilling to come down of his own free will. Whirlwinds blowing across the mountain had been the only force that plucked climbers off the mountain and sent them crashing down with some of their loot to the foot of the mountain.

'The primeheadship of this country is a mountain of wild fleece, my husband,' she continued with a lot of verve. 'It has collected all the wealth of the nation to its top. Whoever is able to climb it has unlimited access to the wild fleece of the country. Our sights are on the mountain of wild fleece and we must climb it. Failing to do so means life at the foot of the mountain where there is barely enough hay to have an animal existence. Living like an animal while knowing you are a human being can be very depressing and painful. I will hang myself first before I accept to live such a life.

'Mountain of wild fleece,' intoned Merima. Yes, he could faintly remember reading about such a mountain in a collection of myths and allegories while at college. But until now, he had never related the mountain of wild fleece with power in Bivan's house.

Now that his wife had done so, the myth or allegory captured quite aptly the condition of Bivan's house. Virtually every office of consequence in the country was a mountain of wild fleece whose wealth was the personal property of the head of the office. No one left high office unless he was forced to. The country's constitution provided for two terms of six years each for the offices of the primehead and big feast. It was thought the terms were long enough to create contentment in holders of these offices so that they would bow out gracefully when their terms were over. But because such offices were mountains of wild fleece there had been successive attempts to amend the country's constitution to increase the terms either to three consecutive terms of five years each or two consecutive terms of seven years each. The various attempts to amend the constitution to increase the primehead's and big feast's tenure in office had failed not because of any principled opposition by the house of archery, but because of the desire of archers to become big feasts and primeheads themselves. Increasing the terms of primehead and big feasts meant postponement of their own ambition to a later date that might not find them alive. So each time a move was made by a primehead to prolong his stay in power through a constitutional amendment, the move was blocked by the house of archery or as some people said, shot down by the archers.

'Even with all the perks and perquisites of public office in this country, I can't understand why no one wants to leave his seat for another person to sit on?' Merima heard himself saying aloud. 'Like the primehead and big feasts who don't want to leave when their time is up, old men in the civil service holding positions of consequence keep changing their age to avoid having to retire from service on grounds of age. Why can't people leave their seats for others?'

'Because they won't find other seats,' said the wife. 'Remember there are no seats at the foot of the mountain of wild fleece. Who can afford to stand for the rest of his life, particularly in old age?' No one wants to go to the gate because there are snakes waiting for you at the gate. If you retire, there is neither gratuity nor pension for you. So the snakes of hunger and destitution will be waiting for you at the gate when you retire so that they can escort you home.'

'Are you sure the snakes at the gate are only snakes of hunger and destitution? I think I can also see snakes of selfishness and greed.'

'I even see more snakes at the gate than those you are seeing.'

'If some people live twice in their jobs, others will live twice out of jobs.

'That's true,' said the wife. 'But Bivan's house will always be Bivan's house. We can't change it. But we can leave where we are at the foot of the mountain and climb up; and that's what we must do. The whore and the ass must take us up the mountain.'

'Yeah, the whore and the ass. The whore and the ass for now seem to be doing more of PLM's, no, Jamimi's, bidding because without him there will be no PLM. How are you getting on with mobilization of the women?'

'I am doing the best I can,' said the wife. 'But you know how women are. Often, we are merely the echoes of our husbands' voices. Unity of spouses in most cases means the dissolution of the woman into the man. In the last meeting of the south-west women, every woman was given a task of winning at least one person into the UAC every day and charging the newly recruited to do same.'

'I like your Jehovah Witness' approach to the matter,' said Merima. 'On my part, I am employing a trick that seems to be working. I have distributed letters of appointment as ceremonial feasts or close banquets to about two hundred men that can deliver their areas to us on the condition that they will only get appointed if they did not show their appointment letter to anyone. Right now each of these two hundred men has thrown himself into my campaign and seems even to be working harder than myself to ensure I win. That's the magical effect of interest. If blood is thicker than water, interest is thicker than blood.'

'Believe me Your Excellency, nothing can be smarter than this!' Merima's wife said, excitedly. 'If you want labor, put a good price on it and the hands of men would never slacken on the plough. You can sell any scam in this country because there is so much greed around to buy it. In the heads of clever people, there is always a spring to the ocean of success. Press hard on this spring and you may not need to claw your way up the mountain of wild fleece. The spring will catapult you there.'

'Yeah,' Merima drawled. 'How does the air feel today on your cheeks? What is the air telling the cheeks of my queen today?'

'What do you mean by what is the air telling my cheeks?'

'How the air presses against your cheeks tells you something about what is coming that day. It is called airology.'

'There is always a crackbrain proposing some crack idea and there are always eccentrics to buy into it.'

'You might be right. But I tell you, there is intelligence in the air. Indeed, the air is intelligence itself. It is solid bodies, solid masses that have no intelligence. But intelligence is always in the air. The mind is air. That's why intelligence lives in it. The heart is a body. That's why only feelings can be found there. Air is a market you can buy intelligence. If you must buy anything, buy intelligence in the air.'

'What does the intelligence in the air says about how matters stand with our hang up?'

'It says now the wind is against us. But it will soon change direction.'

'If I want to buy intelligence in the air on how matters stand with our obsession, how do I do so?'

'Simple. Sit quietly inside your room or in the bush and soak your head in the air,' said Merima. When his wife did not say anything in response to what he had said, he went on, 'If you must buy intelligence on our enterprise, buy it in the air.'

'Buy,' murmured Merima's wife. 'After bruising your head, the whore of the sovereign seems to have placed your mind in the market.'

'Anyone who wants to prosper in the world of today must have his heart in the market. So here the whore has done no harm. It's not only my mind that is in the market. Everyone and everything including choice are up for sale. Everyone is sold on the market. The invisible hand is winning against everyone and everything. Today the market explains everything. It even explains God. The market is indestructible because it is invisible. Invisibility and indestructibility are what make the market divine. We are all sieged by the market. If you mean me to win this election you must have your mind in the market where the voters' votes and God reside.'

'Some of the things you say sound blasphemous to me.'

'These days, we don't know whether blasphemy is a sin against God or the market. Well, let's leave the market for now. Right now, what I want is a good bath. Please, can you set up a bath for me? All these days I

have been on the campaign tumble, I haven't
had a good bath.'

'That's the problem. Since you left on
campaign, there has been no light and water.
For the past two days we have been buying
water.'

Chapter Nine

Whenever things got too depressing in politics, Merima resorted to hunting to recover his humor. The freshness of the air in the forest and the quietness of nature around him were so soothing and pleasing to him that he always felt like a child in the lullaby of his mother whenever he was in the forest. Sometimes he felt like remaining in the forest and never returning home again. On any day he felt this way, he was liable to return home late from the forest. His wife never liked his love for hunting and any day he returned late from the forest, she was liable to whine. But the good cheer he used to return from the forest in used to take the wind out of her anger.

The forests he hunted in were way out of town. In his Range Rover, it normally took him over an hour to get to any of the forests he hunted in. He hunted with only his two dogs as companions and sometimes without them. This was the thing that alarmed his wife more than anything else. If he comes to harm in the forest, who would make a report back home? Much as she pressed him to always go to the forest with another person, he refused.

Going to the forest with someone would deny him the solitude he went there to seek he always told her. He wanted quiet in the forest and a human being would talk. Often, speech was something he found detestable in people. Without speech, there would have been more thought and more action. People would have lived more in their heads than in their mouths. But thinking they are better off with speech, people always make a nuisance of themselves by talking. Man's condition worsened in the tower of Babel where many languages were created. Speech should have simply been taken away from men. In the forest, even if a human being with him did not speak, his mere presence was prone to be resentful to him. It was the shadows of trees he wanted to hug him in the forest, not those of men.

The siege of UAC secretariat in Hatto depressed Merima into going for hunting in Baaku forest. He broke away from the campaign feigning illness and came home from where he set out for the forest. It was going to be counterproductive if he continued the campaign feeling the way he was. Campaign is about wooing people to get them support you. In his current sour mood, he could not court anyone. Rather he felt like yelling at people.

He set out for the forest while rain that started an hour ago was still falling. There was no sun. The sun was behind the rain and mist pelting and soaking the earth. Nothing enlivens him like rain. Whenever rain was falling, he felt like a child again. Like a child, he always wanted to be out of doors whenever it was raining. One of the horrors of hell to him was that they say rain does not fall there.

In the outskirts of the town, the rain began to fall less. Along the highway, the sun burst out on the rain. 'The devil is beating his wife,' he murmured. His father once told him that whenever it is raining and the sun is shining, it means the devil is beating his wife.

Half way to the forest, the rain petered into drizzles. The sky was spiting like a pregnant woman or as if it were suffering a heartburn. With the driver's glass lowered, he occasionally stuck his left hand out of the window to feel the cool breeze that came with the rain and the spits of the sky. He imagined the sky belching before spiting on him whenever a raindrop fell on his hand.

'Heaven has really pissed down today like it has not in a long while,' he said to himself. 'Today the sky must have eaten something very sour to go on spiting like this long after the rain,' he murmured and breathed in as if to inhale the smell of what the sky ate. 'The quiet even before I get to the forest is so refreshing and calming. What am I looking for in this two-faced business called politics? In what way has it made my life richer? Ahh... I am so much involved with others that I will die without meeting myself, knowing who I am or realizing who I am. This ghostly game! This game of masquerades! Yes, politics is a game of ghosts. To be a politician you must die as a man and resurrect as a ghost. There is no one that is his true self in the game because it is a game of appearances and not of reality. A politician is expected to smile even if he is crying inside. His true face is always wearing a mask because the mask is more pleasing to people than the real thing. Whoever wants to live his life outside himself should become a politician. At the university people thought I would provide an intellectual harvest to mankind but the drought of politics like a herbal vampire has sucked all the sap in me leaving straws and withes behind.

When he was about to join politics, a friend had told him he was about to sacrifice the noble principles he was known for and he had agreed with his friend. 'I will leave principles with you,' he had said to the friend. 'Please, take care of them for me. When I return, if I ever, I will take them off you.'

There is no creature that crawls out of its skin so smoothly like the snake, he was now thinking. Politicians do something like that when they crawl out of themselves to play politics. Therefore, politicians are snakes. But they are worse than snakes because snakes are not known to smite each other. There is nothing a politician delights in like smiting another politician. Success in the game in fact entails smiting a fellow to death. Even those who are not politicians, but want to dine and wine with politicians must first become pigs, if they must return to their beds after the dinner. What am I pissing and farting around with politics for? Forest man you are suffering from the diabetes and diarrhoea of ambition.

He was driving along the forest now. Driving on the road's shoulder, when he got to where he could drive completely off the road into the forest, he eased the Range Rover off the road and drove into the forest to a point where from the road no one could see the car. He parked under a cluster of trees where he had once parked. The devil was still beating his wife; but he seemed to be beating her less now. He reclined his seat and lay back to wait for the rain to stop. When it was over, he came down to begin his hunt or his leisure because he seldom shot anything. Out of the car, a slight wind caressing his face and the green forest in his full view affected him in a visibly pleasurable manner. Here, the air was in the air and the ground was on the ground. Out there, things did not always fall into place. There was always a missing sum. It was different here. Here, there was no missing sum and everything was always where it should be.

Today, he was in the forest without his dogs. With his gun in his hand, he began walking the forest looking for game with the ease and familiarity of use, but without the finesse of professionalism. He was so engrossed with the forest and any game he might happen upon that thoughts of politics, his creeping failure to realize his intellectual potentials, were all banished from his mind. He was getting so fused with the forest that he shared its rhythm and heartbeat. Whenever he got so absorbed by the forest, he ceased to be conscious of himself, the gun in his hand and even the forest that so absorbed him or perhaps more appropriately the forest he had so absorbed. In such a state, the games he had come to hunt might gambol past him and he would not see them. He was the forest man carrying the forest and all the games in it inside him and so could not see them, though he might feel them. In this trance-like state the gun sometimes slipped out of his hand and fall on the ground bringing him back to himself. Now he was slipping into a trance and everything around him was giving way to the forest slipping into him. Two grass-cutters raced past him, but he did not see them. It was like they or the forest had cast a spell over him to chain the hunter in him. His eyes fixed and unblinking was cast over the forest which was rushing into him. It was when the gun fell from his hand that he came back to where he was standing. He shook his head and a new look of satisfaction and pleasure overran his face. 'This is it,' he murmured. 'It is almost like coupling with the forest. Ah...man; your wife should not hear this. Else she will set this forest ablaze. But forest-man this is really something. Each time always seems better than the last. The forest has cleaned up the vomit of politics inside me.'

He began moving deeper and deeper into the forest, now more as a hunter on the prowl than the forest freak he was moments ago. He came by a whiff of grasses strewn on the ground like fodder a horse missed out. 'The wind must have rested here,' he murmured. It was his belief that whenever the wind was blowing, it used to pause and rest at some place before moving on. In the forest, he easily recognized places the wind rested in its movement. Usually, those places were scrubby and pale. The wind usually fed on them before moving on. In the place he was now, the wind not only fed on the grasses, it left its teeth behind as evidence of its sojourn. It also left behind a ghostly atmosphere that was pressing heavily upon him.

Near a little stream, he saw an alligator moving leisurely away from the stream towards him. He quickly ducked behind a tree and watched the alligator approaching him. The grace and elegant movement of the alligator excited him. The alligator might have a rough and broken skin but its movement was smooth and wholesome. Half way towards him from the stream, the alligator halted its movement, its eyes darting around. It had sensed his presence. Telepathy is not only a human intelligence; animals too enjoy it, he thought. A bird chirped behind him. He turned and saw it sitting high up the branch of a tree. It was a big bird with a very colorful plumage. 'Such a tiny voice from so big a bird,' he murmured. 'The fat in it is choking its voice.' He turned to look at the alligator, but it was no longer where it was a while ago. It was not even in sight. He looked about him in fear. For all he did not know, it might be about climbing up him, taking him for a tree. Ants do that. Why not alligators? There were stories of hungry pythons swallowing up the legs of hunters who went to sleep in the forest. But the alligator was nowhere near him. What sort of hunter was he, he wondered and laughed. It was not a loud laughter, but it was loud enough to make the alligator lying under a shock of shrubs to stir. He saw the movement and without thinking pulled the trigger. The bullet ripped open the back of the alligator to lie on its belly. That he shot the alligator was not so much due to the accuracy of his marksmanship as to the precision a wild aim sometimes gives to the erring hand of bad shots. The alligator broke cover, whirled round for some time before nodding its head a couple of times, the way a lizard greeting the sun does, only that in the case of the alligator it was not greeting the sun, but bowing to the staff of death. The alligator died, not on its belly, but on its back. Merima thought its dying posture awkward and undignified. Only *menkans* like dying on their backs and they do so to hide a hole on their backs. Was the alligator trying to hide its broken skin? He moved closer to the alligator. Even though dead, he suffered a little revulsion when taking hold of the reptile. He had a phobia for reptiles and rodents. But he had won a trophy and he had to carry it home. Someone needed to know his hand was steady even when it was being pushed.

In some respects, politics and hunting are two sides of the same coin - the kill-coin, he thought. Hunters hunt for animals, politicians for men. Hunters kill only animals. They do not kill fellow hunters. But politicians kill not only fellow politicians but even the electorates. Hunters share their kill throughout the village. Politicians eat theirs alone.

'Alligator are you a politician?' he murmured, his eyes pecking the alligator. 'Were you running away from the fart and piss that drove me to this forest? Poor alligator. Poor me. In a way I share death with you because we are one in the search of escape from the outrages of an obscene game and when one of two that are one dies, a part of the one living dies with his soul-mate. Obscene. Politics is truly an obscene game. What makes it obscene? The nakedness and vulgarity of telling others to allow one rule them must be obscene to any moral and civil being. Power which politics delivers is even more obscene among moral and civil beings. However, in Bivan's house full of moral primates and moral renegades, the vulgar use of public funds to erect private mansions and buy exotic cars upsets no one; nauseates no one. Rather people snuggle to the vulgar. Vulgarity has become a measure of good taste here. The primehead is using public money to acquire private property in broad daylight, but the obscenity of his action neither embarrasses him nor angers the people robbed before their eyes. Somebody said when the primehead dies his greed should be buried in a separate grave so that it does not rise with him on the Day of Judgment to testify against him. The poor are sleeping on the streets and feeding with flies on dustbins and it is normal. Why is everything so naked and obscene here?

He covered the alligator with leaves and moved further into the forest. He still hadn't had enough of the forest and hunting. There was so much forest behind Jonka Palace the official residence of the primehead of Bivan's house. If he becomes primehead, that was where he would hunt day and night. The forest behind the palace perhaps more than anything in Jonka palace excited him.

Chapter Ten

Coming out of his house to begin a campaign trip to Wandugu, Jamimi met an army of people he knew to be largely made up of political spongers and beggars waiting for him inside the premises of his house. Among this army of people was a young man Jamimi had always seen following them since the campaign began. By his appearance, he looked every inch a political sponger. Jamimi called him aside and asked him what he was doing for a living.

'Politics,' answered the young man.

'But politics is not a trade or a profession like carpentry or bricklaying.'

'For me it is. In fact, it is the only trade I know. I have no other business than politics.'

'What do you do in this business?'

'Sponging. You know politics and sponging are Siamese twins - they walk together and sleep together. No one can separate them.'

'I think you are in the wrong party. You should have joined UAC. They have the kind of money you need.'

'UAC is full. There is no space for me there.'

'Do you know you are a layabout, a bum?'

'A bum... No, I think I am smart.'

Seeing he would not get anywhere with the young man, Jamimi left him alone and proceeded on his campaign.

'Bivan's house is fading out of the human picture,' Jamimi began his campaign in Wandugu, standing on a campaign platform made for him. 'There is a walking-world map that follows the world in whichever direction it titters or soars. I checked that map before coming here and I did not see Bivan's house. Even in weather forecasts, no one mentions Bivan's house these days. Why? Because we do not count to the world. Greed and corruption have made us not to count. Greed and corruption: the two warlords in Bivan's house that yield only to themselves are wiping out the country from the regard of the rest of the world. Greed whispers to corruption and corruption wields the machete against everyone. Like termites, corruption has eaten up the fabric of the ceiling that was to shield Bivan's house from the rain and the sun. Like rats, corruption has nipped away the cloth that was meant to cover the nakedness of Bivan's house.' But why is Bivan's house raped and looted by the piss and wind in power and we keep watch and do nothing? I think it is because most members of Bivan's house are morally dead. Check out the history of looting. Looting had always taken place where people were dead. For example, looting followed the volcanic eruption of Mount Bembe. With people dead, felons and miscreants made away with the belongings of the people with no one to raise a switch against them. We have suffered volcanic eruption of corruption here. That's what killed our morality. Greed and corruption are the volcanic eruptions that had reduced this house to ashes and dust! The UAC government is a lake of greed and corruption that is licking and drowning the country. PLM is the spillway that will drain it out of office!'

'The Talking-Secretariat!' someone shouted into Jamimi's speech.

'No, you should have said the secretary bird that feeds on snakes - your snakes,' someone close to the man who spoke into Jamimi's speech, said.

'Rhetoric is always sweet outside power, but sour inside it,' said the man who was presumed to be a UAC supporter.

'His rhetoric does not resonate with me,' said another seeming UAC supporter. 'It's not only Bivan's house that is being looted. The whole world is being looted by the modern industry. Our taste for industrial goods has released termites and locusts upon the earth.'

'As a spin doctor for UAC, you need more craft and training,' someone said.

'Nothing happens here when it should,' somebody lamented. 'A meeting slated for 2p.m may not get underway until 4p.m Not keeping to time is a sign that promises made to anyone will not be kept.'

'Elsewhere people are living out their dreams. In Bivan's house, we are living out our nightmare. Thanks to the malfunctioning heart that is the government of Boyama,' Jamimi continued after a momentary pause. 'This malfunctioning heart does not circulate blood around the body of Bivan's house. That is why the body is dying. We must remove the UAC malfunctioning heart by a switch surgery. PLM is the sure-fire that will burn up the UAC mess. Like sharks, Boyama and Merima the UAC anointed heir need to push their stomachs out and wash them clean of the public money they had eaten. If they will not, we will do so for them.'

'His words are warm-fuzzies to me,' someone said.

'They are a warm-over to me,' said a UAC supporter. 'I heard something like this the other day from Jamimi.'

'We are sieged by the death of values,' Jamimi continued after another pause. 'We are sieged by meaninglessness. We are so drunk with the greed and corruption the UAC government has infected us with that we are ready to eat tomorrow today. Where are the oracles of Bivan's house? Have they been bribed not to speak out against our sunk condition? Yesterday people earned good names and honor with integrity. But today integrity is no longer the currency honor and a good name are bought. Honor and a good name are now bought with money. Public thieves are chiefs now. Shame now is not for the thief, but for he who is poor because he can't steal. Money meant for water supply and power generation is stolen by those in government. There is no water, there is no light. People can barely feed because food is so expensive. Yet, people can't link their poverty to the wealth of those stealing money meant for them. Rather at wedding ceremonies, town meetings and even funeral ceremonies, the poor people cheer those who pauperize them. Whoever can dole out money is a god people worship. Forget all this show of church and mosque attendance. It is all farce. The only thing Bivan's house members worship now is money and whoever has it. That is why there is this mad rush for money.'

'The whole world is under siege,' said a UAC supporter. 'It's not only Bivan's house that is under siege. Food and glitter have laid siege on the world. Things that were thought in the morning to be solutions to the problems created by food and glitter have in the evening become problems – sometimes bigger problems than those they were earlier thought to be solutions for. Yet, no one is ready to shut down his stomach or rein back his taste. The whole human race is turning round and round in an uncoordinated gyre to find a hole to enter and be safe, but it seems there is no hole nearby or even far at. As for our obsession with money, how is UAC to blame? Did UAC bring money and the market that demands money from us?'

'As a man who would die with the UAC, you are getting closer to your grave,' said a PLM supporter standing close to the UAC supporter. 'Take this,' he said, clubbing the UAC supporter hard on the head. The UAC supporter fell down only to be kicked and trampled on by other PLM supporters.

'Choice is the bedrock of happiness,' continued Jamimi, oblivious of a man being trampled to death in his rally. 'This is what we are denied by the UAC during elections. I tell you, those who succeed in life are those who insist on making their own choices. As with individuals it is with nations. Nations that succeed are those that make their own choices. Members of Bivan's house who are in fact the nation called Bivan's house must insist on making their own choice in the next election. The people's choice and consent make leaders to arise out of the people. The fraud and force of those with power make rulers to arise over the people. When leaders arise out of the people, they lead in respect of the people. When rulers arise over the people, they rule in contempt of the people.

'The youths in particular must wake up to their responsibility. The youths are the people whose tomorrows are more than their yesterdays. They must not allow people whose yesterdays are more than their tomorrows desecrate their tomorrows. Leaders work for those who chose them. It is naive to think Boyama will choose your leader for you and the leader will work for you and not for Boyama that chose him. The first responsibility of a child is to his father and mother. It is foolish to sell your vote and expect the person who bought your vote to still serve you. It is like selling your millet at the market and expecting the person who bought the millet to make porridge with it and share with you. Now we are having power on our backs instead of beside us. Why? Because like the donkey which cannot choose its owner, we have not been choosing our leaders. Whatever men have tamed, they regard not. Look at the sheep and the dog; how much regard do they receive from men. Look at the tiger and the lion, how much regard do they receive from men? To what have we sold our present and our future? To lies and dishonesty. Any wonder why our fortunes are what they are? Lies and dishonesty are empty oil wells and whoever invests in them can only drill barrels of hot air. The more politicians eat your money, the more they become mealy mouthed and the more they look mealy during campaigns. Look at UAC and you will understand what I am saying.

'The Peoples Liberation Movement is the cure to the UAC disease,' Jamimi continued in a high-pitched voice after a momentary pause. 'We have a track record in public service that supports our claim of being a cure. For your own good and the good of your offspring, you must not only vote for PLM in the forthcoming elections, you must insist that your vote is counted and that it counts. Only PLM will bring this great nation back into the center of the world-walking map. PLM!'

There was a thunderous shout of 'justice' from the crowd.

Holding the microphone tightly, Jamimi began to sing and shuffle his feet on the campaign platform:

> Water is gushing out from a rock
> Water is gushing out from a rock
> Whoever drinks he shall be saved
> Whoever drinks he shall be saved
> I drank of it and I am saved
> Whoever drinks he shall be saved

'What a transformation!' exclaimed Nkume who was at the campaign rally. 'Jamimi in politics and doing so well. What a transformation!'

'I have always known he will be a political asset if only he would develop interest in the game,' said Bobi who was also at the rally.

'You remember that poem he wrote back in school?' asked Nkume.

'You know I have no heart for poetry,' answered Bobi who seemed to be paying more attention to what Jamimi was saying than the distraction Nkume was drawing him into.

'Rather than not having a heart for poetry, I think you have no head for it,' said Nkume. 'Interestingly, the poem I am talking about is *The Return of my Heart* in which Jamimi paid tribute to the lady of his heart.'

'What has that poem to do with the business before us?'

'Jamimi is the return of politics to Bivan's house as Jiro was the return of Jamimi's heart. Can't you see?'

'Politics is truly a cloak-and-dagger game,' said an old man standing near Nkume and Bobi. 'Fighting for people's favors, politicians are ever ready to stick the knife into the guts of their opponents.'

'One part of his spin deceived me but the other didn't,' said the man standing near the old man. 'All politicians are mealy mouthed. Which politician ever speaks to you on the level and on fair regard? A politician who has never been to church for more than three years the other day was in church and said without batting an eyelid that he was unashamed of his deep faith.'

'Water, food and light are still problems with us when elsewhere they are taken for granted,' Jamimi went on. 'Even cities that used to have pipe borne water, the taps no longer flow and where they do, the water is filthy and a sure vector for typhoid. In the rainy season, town and village folks rely on rain for drinking water. At night Bivan's house is one big forest of darkness dotted here and there by specks and flares of electric light where the Electricity Board wants to remind us that it still exists. The UAC government of Boyama believes we are dead and dead people need no light. Whoever heard of a clamor for light in a cemetery? As for security of life and property the poor of this country have little to worry over. Having no property, they have little to fear from the armed robber. If out of sadism an armed robber kills a poor man, unknown to him he might be doing mercy killing.

'Now is the time for change and you are the instruments of change. Come out and dare the guns of Boyama. In our situation you either die on the street by a bullet of the oppressor or by hunger and misery in your house. You either die at once on the street or by installments in your house. You either die with honor while seeking to reclaim your right or like a dog clubbed to death by dog-eaters. Violent death has become a creeping certainty for most members of Bivan's house. You will not die when you face the oppressor because the oppressor is like a hyena. The hyena is a coward even though it may bare its teeth at you. Often when it bares its teeth at you, it does so out of cowardice. If you bare your own teeth, it will flee. Afflicted by a guilty conscience, the oppressor is always afraid. The strength of the oppressor lies in your lack of protest, in your lack of fight. Lies prevail and are hailed in town only before the arrival of truth. As soon as truth turns up, lies do not sneak away, they take to their heels. When out of fear and docility you make your hand so impotent that you can't raise it against the oppressor, you give potency to the hand of the oppressor to squeeze out your life blood. When by courage you give potency to your arm, you make the arm of the oppressor impotent and so you pummel him as you like. Your destiny does not make you. You make your destiny. I am now in Wandugu. No amount of prayer and wishful thoughts would have brought Wandugu to me. I had to enter a train and be brought here. Whatever you want, you have to work for it. That's what I see in life. As you make your bed so shall you lie on it. If you make a royal bed, you will lie on a royal bed. If you make a pauper's bed, you will lie on a pauper's bed. You cannot make a pauper's bed and expect another person to lie on it or even share it with you. Without exception, we are all what we worked for in life.

'PLM will bring back water and light to this country,' Jamimi enthused after a brief pause. 'There will be medicine in the hospitals and the death-trap roads will be replaced with good roads. PLM will do these because Jamimi as primehead will ensure that no one steals public money meant to provide these public services to the people.'

There were prolonged loud shouts of adulation from the crowd.

'In the coming general elections, with your vote you can make or mar the fortunes of this great country,' Jamimi continued. 'We make the fortunes of this country when we vote for PLM and ensure that our votes are counted and that they count. We mar the fortunes of this nation when we vote for UAC, when we neglect to vote or when we vote for PLM, but do not ensure the sanctity of our votes is respected by the fraudulent UAC government. PLM!'

'Justice!' cried the crowd.

'I think Jamimi is not holding the whole picture of our situation before the people,' said Bobi when Jamimi came to the end of his long speech. 'I think he is not telling the whole story.'

'What do you mean by Jamimi not holding the whole picture before the people?' asked Nkume. 'Where is the whole picture and what is the whole story?'

'This is the whole picture and the whole story,' said Bobi, his face free of the earlier amusement Nkume saw on it. 'It is not only leaders that are irresponsible as Jamimi seems to think. We are all irresponsible people in this country. Leadership is irresponsible because the followership is irresponsible. The followership is irresponsible because the leadership is irresponsible. It is only in this country that no one pays tax and so no one can say he is a contributor to the national wealth of the nation. There is no money you can refer to as *tax payers' money* in this country. This country to me is a bank. However, it is not the conventional bank you know, but a strange kind of bank. In this bank, when you look at the desk of the receiving cashier, there is no queue of customers paying in money. However, if you look at the desk of the paying cashier, there is a long queue of people shoving each other to be paid money they did not pay in. Because the Bank is only paying, but never receiving, it will soon go bankrupt. This country is a society of hunters and not of farmers. In a society of farmers, people pay tax to the soil - they till the soil and plant their crops which they harvest during the season of harvest. But in a society of hunters, no one pays tax. Hunters go out with their bows and arrows, sticks, catapults, spears and guns to shoot wild animal they do not know how they came to be in the forest. Those with guns and great hunting skills are likely to return home with more games than those with mere sticks and poor hunting skills. Those with poor hunting skills knowing they did not breed the animals that were shot, dared not challenge the great hunters that are about exhausting the animals in the forest. In a society of farmers, let anyone dare go to the community farm and harvest all the crops to his barn and see what the response of the other farmers would be.'

'You have a point there,' said Nkume, sounding cheerless. 'We are a society of freeloaders, free-riders and freewheelers. That's why we are in for a free fall in everything. But if you take a closer look at the whole picture you have placed before us, you will find that leadership is still to be blamed for the irresponsibility of followership.'

'How?'

'We were paying taxes before. Who abolished the taxes? Leadership. Looking at the matter now, perhaps they abolished taxes to produce the result we are now lamenting. Being irresponsible, leadership seeks to breed irresponsibility in the followership; being corrupt, it seeks to nurture corruption in the followership so that its own corruption would not be seen. Government anywhere has the responsibility of nurturing positive values in the people. People in government should not only live in high places, they should live on the highest moral ground. If Jamimi gets power, he must live on such moral ground that inspires responsibility in our people.

'Things can really be funny,' said Bobi. 'When taxes were abolished, the poor thought a lot of good was being done to them. Little did they know or even suspect that the abolition of taxes was meant to make them voiceless and impotent.'

'You know it is the same thing with the cow,' said Nkume. 'When the cow is being fattened, it thinks it is being done a lot of good. Little does it know or even suspect it is being fattened for slaughter. The devil often appears like an angel of light.'

Chapter Eleven

The PLM campaign train was travelling at sixty kilometers per hour when it went off the track while negotiating a bend. The train plunged into the forest like an angry bull charging after the source of its annoyance. From a distance the train ripping through the forest was a very frightening and amazing spectacle. The train sailed through the forest like a grass snake for about fifty meters before it collided with a huge tree and its different coaches twisted out of its long trunk in a grotesque tableau. People on top of the train either jumped down - some to their death, or were thrown clear or under the train when it fell on its side. Moments after hitting the tree and falling on its side, the train burst into flames. First, the wind puffed a little flame which flared unsteadily for a while like a drunken man lopping home before sinking its teeth into the grass like a shark into a sea seal.

Screams and squeals of people in wild terror of what was happening burst out of the train in a long, hollow pitch of fear and shock. The forest full of dry grass was kindling that fuelled the fire into a big inferno. Later it was found there were ditches in the forest into which petrol was poured. It was the petrol in the dug ditches that ignited the derailed train. The fire ripped through the coaches as if they were not of metal but of tinder. People lucky to be near windows or doors that were up in the air jumped out of the raging inferno - some of them on fire. Two cattle herdsmen who happened to be nearby when the train went off the track were so concerned with the safety of their cattle to be of any help. Before the train burst into flames, they had hung around in shock and bewilderment hoping to be of help. But when it burst into flames, they began driving their cattle quickly away from the wild fire.

Grasshoppers leaping after insects suddenly found fire leaping after them not with the inert limbs of frogs leaping out of water, but with the nimbleness of swooping hawks. Jets of smoke and flames billowed out of the burning train in fiery and liquid rivulets that licked anything on their path. Tears and splinters of fire leapt out of the train like birds with broken wings, flared for a while in midair before falling to the ground when they could no longer hang in the air. Blades and looms of fire flared and scoured through the forest like rioting maniacal imps. A pall of smoke hung over the forest as if it were stranded with nowhere to go. A man holding a little boy of about four years tore out of the train, both on fire and rolled on the ground in an effort to put out the fire still more on his clothes than on his flesh. A woman in only her undies fell off the flaming train her hands flailing about her trying to cut off spikes and sheets of flames that were clinging to her in a deliberate, uncanny manner. Those trapped inside the flaming wreckage were screaming and howling for help as they roasted to death in the raging inferno.

When the fire was over - after burning for over an hour, hell like a rampaging tornado appeared to have touched down and folded back into the skies again where the train crashed - leaving behind it a charred scroll. Vultures from far and near looking like they were vomited by the fire hung about in the air and on nearby trees like fell angels waiting to take the dead home. Some of the morbid angels from inferno lolled about with a lethargy that was characteristic of carrion eaters - a lethargy they seemed to seep from the dead. Charred remains of human beings lay strewn all over the long stretch of the singed train. Curiously, very few dead human bodies were found inside the scorched train. It was like the train having roasted a person to death threw him out for the vultures hovering above.

Survivors of the train crash were at different spots of the massive forest groaning in pains and crying for help. But the crash took place in a far-flung forest near which there was no human habitation. A railtrack being not a motorway, there was little hope that it would bring help to the surviving victims of the crash soon – more so that rail transportation in Bivan's house had packed up completely. Because trains were not running, even the track repair trolleys that used to run the tracks tightening loose nuts and fixing disjointed planks were rarely seen on the tracks. The two herdsmen seeing that their cattle were safe from the fire came back to help surviving victims of the crash, but there was little they could do beyond showing sympathy and carrying to shades of trees those that were lying in the sun because they could not move.

The driver of the train had perished in the crash, but his assistant, a slim, long-jawed man, had survived. By a tree he was nursing his right leg which seemed to be broken by the way he was holding it. He was holding the leg with both hands as if it were something loose that would fall apart if he released his hold. Beads of sweat were gathered on his forehead, but he could not take one hand off the leg to clear the sweat on his forehead. Instead he wiped the face against his shoulder biting his lips apparently in response to a stab of pain shooting through the injured leg. Apart from the pain from his leg, the shock of the crash was an additional source of anguish. Without warning the train had run into a gash where the railtrack had been cut off. In his more than twenty-eight years' service in the railway corporation, he had never seen anything like this. There was nothing the driver could do to save the train from crashing the way it did. Who could have removed the rail bar from the railtrack he kept asking himself? From the way the soil where the rail bar was removed had been turned up, it was clear that the bar was forcefully removed that day or the evening of the previous day and it was removed for the purpose it has accomplished. In his mind he had no doubt who did this. For more than twenty-three years no train has been running the railtracks of Bivan's house until PLM came up with the novelty of campaigning by train. Part of the reason people were always by the railtrack to welcome the PLM train was the nostalgia of seeing a train moving again. It was only the UAC he knew that was angry with the PLM campaigning by rail. So, this must be the handiwork of the UAC. They must have intended to perish both the train and those in it including Jamimi. But as it turned out, Jamimi was not even on the train. Jamimi had influenza. Not to worsen it, he had decided to travel to Babika by road instead of rail. The train always stirred up a lot of dust particularly when it was moving through any of Bivan's house's mountains of refuse.

Politics! Who said we can be politicians with this impolitic attitude? thought the assistant train driver. What is the matter with our fingers that they soil whatever they touch? Into what have we dipped them? Our hearts are not right. So our minds can't manage well what is working for others.

At different parts of the forest, surviving victims of the crash fortunate to still have their cell phones with them were making frantic calls to their relatives and friends telling them about the crash and the distress they had fallen into. The forest was murmuring, and in some cases, resonating with voices of victims speaking with their relatives on their cell phones. 'UAC has decided to fry us in the forest as if we are grasshoppers,' one man kept repeating over his cell phone. 'UAC the children of fire have derailed our train into the forest which they had flooded with fire. Many of us in the train have passed to the great beyond through a gate of fire.'

Curses and abuses fell on the UAC and Boyama with the splattering sound of late-night rain on corrugated zinc. 'You don't go after power like a honey hunter with flames of fire flaring from your smoker scorching your people,' said one of the victims of the crash to no one in particular.

The first help for victims of the crash came towards sunset. However, it did not come from any of the relatives of the crash victims who had been phoned, but from the UAC which was accused of masterminding the crash. The sun having moved close to night, night was beginning to cast its shadow over it and it was surrendering its life to the authority of the night by the pale look on its face. Merima was hunting in the great

Okunno forest when he saw the smoke of the burning train rising into the atmosphere. The smoke was either that of burning tires or a burning bush, he thought. It was common in Bivan's house for tires to be gathered in a heap and burned for the wires inside them. But who would bring tires so far away, he wondered. Usually, tires were burned close to towns and this was way out of town. The smoke was likely to be from a burning bush. The rains had come. But there was still enough fodder in the forest for fire to burn. The great smoke produced by the fire was likely to be because of the partial wetness of the forest. But the season of bushfires when hunters used to torch the forest for games was over. But after the hunters finished burning the forest, farmers also were involved in biomass burning in their farms to provide manure for their crops. In the case of virgin or fallowed lands being prepared for cultivation, there was a lot of biomass burning by farmers in Bivan's house. In the middle of a thick forest, one can suddenly come upon a defiled forest with ghostly trees and a ghostly atmosphere that biomass burning has bred. This was something Merima hated and had always fought against. He had vowed to stamp out the practice of biomass burning by farmers in Bivan's house if he becomes primehead. Now he must investigate the source of this fire. The smoke looked a little far off, but he was determined to reach where the fire was and put it out if he could. He began moving fast towards the high column of smoke. As he moved closer to the source of the smoke, he began hearing the groans and cries of people in grave distress. For a while he halted in his walk towards the smoke. What was the meaning of this? he wondered. From where he was standing, he listened again, craning his ears in the direction of the smoke. What came to him was a distinct cry of anguish from a dying man.

This is big political capital the thought flashed through Merima's mind. At this time when UAC was so down in popularity, booed and jeered wherever it went on campaign, news that the primehead candidate of the party has rescued a dying man in the forest from the jaws of death was sure to shoot up the rating of the party in the minds of the voting public and improve its chances of winning election with less accusations of rigging. But what could have brought a man out here in a forest like this to suffer whatever misfortune he had suffered? Well, what about you? What brought you so far out to see this smoke? But he was a hunting buff. Other people were not necessarily like him.

More cries and groans of agony came to Merima where he was still standing. The eerie sound they produced was much like the song of death the Kiyak tribe followed a corpse to the grave with. Merima's heart contracted in momentary fear. Whenever the Kiyak tribe was walking a corpse to the grave which was always in the forest, whoever they met on the way would have to escort their dead to the great beyond.

The Kiyak practiced smoke burial. Burying their dead in smoke, they said the souls of the departed reached heaven faster. Their procession to the forest with the corpse was marked by smoke. It was said the smoke warned people on their path to flee unless they want to attend to the dead in the great beyond. But the smoke Merima was beholding was not moving and it was too great to be smoke the Kiyak tribe carried with them. What began as an itch in his heart to save the forest from its buccaneers was fast developing into something exciting and sinister. Perhaps the Kiyak tribe had reached where they would bury their dead. They used to kindle a great fire where they would bury their dead. That perhaps was why there was such a great smoke. It would be exciting to crawl forward and watch in hiding this ancient mode of burial. He began to tiptoe forward, his neck and eyes probing long and wide. His eyes like the antennae of a wary cockroach picked up a string of bottles on a rail pole before they picked up the wreckage of the burning train. 'What!' he exclaimed, involuntarily. Immediately, he knew it was the PLM train that had crashed. It was the only train on the railtracks of Bivan's house and so must be the train now burning. Could the UAC chairman or Boyama grown so murderous in their resentment as to have plotted and executed a mischief that caused the train to crash? 'This is terrible!' he exclaimed, shuddering.

'Yes,' it is terrible,' said Buaka one of PLM supporters lucky to survive the crash unscathed. He had moved far off the scene of the crash in search of a stream to fetch water, but did not find any. He was returning from his fruitless search when he saw Merima. At first, he could not believe it was the primehead candidate of the UAC that he was seeing. But he was a man of physics and not of metaphysics. He believed that whatever cannot happen, if he sees it happening, it is not happening. It was either Merima or his look-alike. It could not be a spirit. He favored the man he was seeing to be Merima. But what could the UAC primehead candidate and the likely primehead of Bivan's house be doing in the forest alone? Could he have removed the rail line and was lurking around to see the train actually crashing? Such an act was too low for a primehead candidate. Did some UAC members do it and were lurking around with the primehead candidate savoring the result of their perfidy? He looked round, but saw no one and felt the eyes of no one on him. He was imagining things he murmured to himself. He knew Merima to be a reasonably decent man that would not stoop so low to be part of a plot to derail the PLM train, least be where the plot would be executed. He was one of the few people that knew Merima loved hunting. Perhaps Merima had gone hunting and had stumbled on what had happened. Whatever be the case, Merima deserved his hatred and contempt for being a friend of those who caused the derailment. Should he surprise him with an attack from behind? Merima was armed with a gun and he was not even with a stick. If Merima heard the rush of his attack and spun round shooting that would be that. Even if he managed to close in on him, in a combat, he was sure he stood no chance against Merima. Worse, he did not know how many people survived the crash and were fit to assist him in the event of a fight between him and Merima. He decided to follow the UAC primehead candidate from behind without the latter knowing.

'We have UAC to thank for this terror,' Buaka said, loudly.

Merima spun round to find Buaka following him behind, his face clouded with scorn.

'Are you here to gloat over the havoc your party has wrought once more?' Buaka asked, his voice thick with bile.

'What really happened to cause the train to derail?' Merima asked, ignoring Buaka's scorn and question.

'Merima, cut out this pretense,' Buaka said in his usual loud voice. Come out clean. Stop this show of sympathy and ignorance of the cause of the derailment. We all have heads on our necks and they are not there like balloons on scarecrows.'

Many of the surviving victims of the crash who could walk began walking to where Merima and Buaka were on hearing the name Merima. Even those who could not walk but could crawl, began crawling to where the two men were.

'I admit circumstances entitle you to think the way you do,' said Merima. 'But honestly, as far as I know, my party has nothing to do with this.'

'From what I know of you, you are not exactly a bad guy. So you may be speaking the truth. But your party! Your party is in cahoots with the devil. There was a man I once heard making this confession: "I pray five times every day as required by my religion. But throughout the day, my heart is with the devil." The heart of UAC is with the devil.'

'Well...'

'You can be believed. But how did you turn up so dramatically in a wilderness like this shortly after what has happened if your party has no hand in it?'

'I was hunting a little far off when I saw the smoke. Initially I thought the smoke was from a farmer who was burning trees to create a farm in the forest - something I abhor. I came to see if I can stop the farmer from burning the forest. But as I drew closer, I heard the groaning and crying of people and I thought it was the Kiyak tribe that was burying their dead one. It was only when I saw a rail pole and the burning wreckage of the train that I knew what had happened.'

'We are the Kiyak tribe and you will be buried with our dead,' said one of the people that had gathered around Merima and Buaka.

'No, we are not the Kiyak tribe. We are patriotic members of Bivan's house seeking to move the nation forward,' said Buaka.

'Kill him. What are we doing to ourselves talking to a vermin that will live on our blood?' someone cried.

'He is innocent,' said another person.

'He might be innocent, but he lives on the guilt of his party and he might prosper by it,' said a man standing behind Merima.

'Where is Jamimi?' asked Merima to the surprise of many people.

'He is dead; consumed by the fire of UAC,' someone hoping to stoke the fire of hatred said.

'No, that can't be! Jamimi cannot die like a grasshopper in a bush fire,' cried Merima.

'Unfortunately, that's how UAC wanted him to die,' said the person stoking the fire of hatred. 'When anomie and anarchy are in a country, anyone can die anyway.'

'Oh my God!' Merima cried.

'UAC has no God,' someone hissed. Other people began to speak without observing any form of conversation.

'UAC may have no God, but Merima has a god.'

'Death is an account that leaves behind a sum. Jamimi's life was an account in which he made huge deposits.'

'What's the account of death?'

'The account of death is the note it leaves behind. Every death leaves behind a note on the life of the deceased whether he was good or bad, whether he was a success or a failure.'

'What is the account of life and what is the deposit?'

'The account of life is how it was lived. The deposit is what one achieved.'

'Your life is without account and without deposit because you live for nothing. So if you die, you go with all that you have.'

'Death is a tonic to life. It gives life to life.'

'Death is raw and can only give a raw deal.'

'If ever I see death, I will tell it what the devil forgot to tell it,'

'Death has already seen you and is wondering why it didn't take you with others to the great beyond.'

'You are a man of raw wit. A man of undigested humor and it is no wonder your humor is causing diarrhoea in many stomachs.'

'Instead of standing and talking here, let's find help for those who can still benefit from help,' Merima said and began calling a number from his cell phone. He was calling the station master of Maila railway station to send a railway car to the Okunno forest to carry the injured to the hospital at Maila.

There was a sigh of relief on the faces of many of the injured people. Earlier calls for relief were without much hope of fruition. There was no motorway to where the crash took place and so it could only be accessed on foot, by rail or by air. It was like those who chose to derail the train in the Okunno forest did so deliberately to cut off the victims of the crash from any assistance.

Chapter Twelve

At Babika, Jamimi and Mengo the secretary of the party waited in vain for the campaign train to arrive. There was a two-hour difference between a journey by road and one by rail between Chuwa and Babika. Even though Jamimi and Mengo got to Babika around 1.30 pm, it was about 4pm they began getting worried that the train hadn't arrived Babika. Jamimi had the phone numbers of only two people in the train while Mengo had no one's number. He was supposed to be a politician whose major capital were people, but Mengo was elusive to people. He hardly stored anyone's number in his cell phone. Even the few he stored, he was always changing *Sim* cards and so often he had very few stored numbers in his mobile phone. People calling him and always finding his number not available had given up. Besides being elusive, Mengo was arrogant and full of imperial airs. On a campaign trip by air to the far away city of Ghalin the PLM campaign team landed at Ghalin international airport and was parcelled into vehicles to be conveyed to the city. Mengo was taken to a Peugeot 406 but he protested that it was too lowly a car for him to ride in. Only a Hummer jeep was good enough for him. Of all the PLM national executive members, it was only Mengo that did not subscribe to the idea of campaigning by rail. When the idea was first mooted, he protested vehemently against it calling it antediluvian and energy sapping. But since the primehead candidate and other party executive members were sold on the idea, he had no choice but to back down. When Jamimi complained of contracting influenza because of the train campaign, he smiled secretly to himself. Eventually everyone would see the matter the way he saw it at the beginning. When it was suggested that the primehead candidate travelled to Babika by road, he was the first person to hop into the car with him. He was considered a major weak link in the PLM national executive chain. The party was an opposition party struggling to seize power from the UAC, but already its secretary had bourgeois tendencies that many within the party wondered how he would behave if the party were to seize the reins of power. They were only moving in the direction of Jonka Palace and he was already riding a high horse. What would he ride when they get there?

Jamimi called the numbers of the two people he had their numbers, but the machine kept telling him the numbers could not be reached at the moment. He assumed that the train was then passing through a no-service area. Thirty minutes later, he called the same numbers, but got the same response. He began to call the numbers continuously, but the situation remained the same up till sunset. Generally he was a calm man who rarely showed excitement of any kind. But now it was obvious he was worried. He kept standing up from his seat to pace about the room he and Mengo were. He called his driver hoping he might have the number of someone in the train only for the driver to tell him he lost his cell phone the previous day. Night was fast falling and there was little he could do in the way of finding out what had happened to the train and his party's supporters. It was before him the train left Chuwa for Babika. If the train was anywhere, it was not in Chuwa but between Chuwa and Babika. So going to Chuwa to check would not be useful. There were places in Bivan's house rail lines and roads lay not far off from each other. The rail line and road between Chuwa and Babika however did not lie near each other at any point, but far apart. Now it seemed to him like the rail line between Chuwa and Babika lay in a tunnel of forest that was inaccessible by road or by foot. There was nothing he could do that night, but wait and hope that something awfully bad hadn't happened. As for all things being well, it was not possible that all things would be well.

8 pm was time for network news in Bivan's house. It was then Jamimi learned of the train crash. The newscaster after telecasting the crash went on to say that Jamimi was feared to have died in the crash. In a strange twist of fate, the newscaster said Merima who was hunting nearby was on hand to assist survivors of the crash by taking those injured to hospital and those not injured to their homes.

Jamimi and Mengo were both watching the television when the tragedy was reported. It was so shocking and distressing to Jamimi that despite the weather that was not hot, sweat broke out on his forehead. For a long time he sat staring at the television saying nothing, feeling numb and dizzy. There was no part of the news that he did not find crushing. Was it the fact that his supporters crashed in a train and he was not with them to help them or die with them or the fact that it was his rival that helped them? Was it the roasting to death of people in the train or the fact that he was feared dead in the crash?

From his face it was difficult to tell the effect of the crash on Mengo.

'This is terrible!' Jamimi exclaimed, jumping up from where he was sitting to pace around the room.

'It's indeed terrible,' said Mengo.

'But if indeed anyone survived the crash as the newscaster said, how was it that those who survived were not able to tell the world I was not in the crashed train?' he said half to himself, half to Mengo.

'That's the big wonder. But maybe they were too numb to talk.'

'We have a mess on the floor of our living room.'

'And I don't think either the dog or the pig would be able to eat up this mess.'

'Now, Merima is a hero, a Good Samaritan of sort.'

'And you are now a ghost. Things can't get messier than this. And election is less than two weeks away. If only we didn't get entangled with this train idea.'

'I don't think the idea was a bad one. People flocked to the train. Because your fishing line has caught a frog you say it's a bad thing. What of the many fishes it had caught for you?'

'The first thing we must do is to tell the world you were not roasted in the fire before people start running away from you taking you for a ghost.'

'That's true. But that means I was alive while my supporters were being roasted to death without my coming to their rescue. That I was in a hotel room having my leisure while Merima was rescuing my supporters from an inferno is not commending by any self-serving view. How can we still count on the votes of our supporters rescued by Merima? Unlike a good shepherd, people will say I put my flock into the train and travelled by road to await their arrival - however they make it. If I say this is the only time I travelled by road, mischief would say why was it that only when the train was to crash that Jamimi travelled by road? Such a query you know is pregnant with insinuations.'

'Pregnant,' muttered Mengo, a bemused expression on his face. 'You know someone said, we were once pregnant with development in this country only for UAC to make us suffer a miscarriage. Since then the nation has not been able to conceive again because it is husbanded by impotent leaders. That's by the way. On the issue at hand, if the UAC's query you referred to is pregnant with negative insinuations, we will force it to miscarry. Besides, they are not the only people who can insinuate. Right now I am wondering how improbable it was for Merima to be merely hunting in the neighborhood when the disaster took place. Such a tale sounds like a fairy to me. This is their own pregnant woman and she can deliver a monster they won't like to see.'

'None of these is pleasant to me.'

'We take drugs to cure ailments not because taking them is pleasant. For that matter, there are very few things that are sweet or that we would have preferred to spend our time on that help us along. It's bitter things, things we least like to do that help us along and so we do them to get along and get by.'

'Okunno forest is a huge tank. Where in this gigantic tank did the train crash occur? The newscaster did not say.'

'You have said something there. That forest is a kind of tomb; a tomb that has now swallowed our supporters.'

'I don't like the omen whispering to me out of this tragedy.'

'I can feel something witchery about it. It's like the fire of the crash had eaten out my intestines. I feel hollow inside.' Mengo was getting really concerned. Not out of sympathy for human misery, but out of fear that a single, awful event like this could torpedo them out of the coast of power. There are many slips between the cup and the lips. This could be one of them.

'I don't know whether it is because this country is big; whenever there is a disaster here, it is always big.'

'The fall of the elephant is always mighty.

'Who, what could have derailed the train?'

'Your popularity with the electorates can anger someone to spite. On the road women had spread their wrappers and men their mats for you to drive over - something that reminds me of the rich oil used to clean Jesus' feet.'

'Throughout the ages, women have always had more faith and love than men.'

'Or more emotions.'

'Perhaps so. But you can never charge them with hypocrisy - something men are adept at.'

'The whole thing is so paralyzing to my mind.'

'Do you have a mind? You acquire a mind from books and you read no books. You don't even read newspapers.' If you have any mind, it must be a very small one you acquired from gossips.'

Somebody once said that if you want to know how big your mind is, call a meeting in your mind and see how many spirits will attend. I called such a meeting in my mind recently and it was attended by many spirits.'

'We have a multitude followership and the devil is spinning up a drought to deny us the harvest that is deservedly ours.'

'It is only in politics that a multitude is a good thing. In every other thing, a multitude is bad. There is something poor and beggarly about multitudes.'

'I have two minds now. One mind is saying we should go back to Chuwa this night, the other is saying we should wait till morning.'

'I don't think it is two minds you have. Rather you have two governors - emotions and reason and I can say which is telling you what. Ever present in man over a matter are sentiments and objectivity; lies and truth. Action is a helicopter with two propellers: passion and reason. Any of these propellers can lift up the helicopter. Whether you crash or land safely depends on the propeller that lifted you into the stormy skies. Lies and truth, sentiments and objectivity, emotions and reason. You will find out that the multitude here, the pluralistic here is what is bad. The bad always exist in multitudes.'

'Are you suggesting because the poor are in multitudes, they are necessarily bad?'

'I am not suggesting anything. I am only telling you what to listen to.'

Outside where they were, a choir was singing a very soulful song about Jesus coming to take them home. It was a song Jamimi sang as a child, a song he hadn't heard a long time off. Like a small band of soldiers besieged by a large army, by their song, the chorister seemed to hope for a miraculous delivery from the jaws of death they were.

It is the inalienable right of their sentiments to hope for the best against all the odds. But it is the duty of their reason to prepare for the worst,' said Mengo.

'That song connects me with life again,' said Jamimi. 'How I wish Jesus comes now. There is no better time for him to come than now that things are upside down. I am very much desirous of being taken home now.'

'I can hear salvation whispering a tearful song into your ears.'

Outside, the choristers had stopped singing. Had Jesus taken them home? The void left behind by the choristers was filled by the wind. Outside the wind hummed, buzzed and seethed as if it were pregnant with a monster.'

Inside Jamimi was agonizing over the train crash. He scarcely slept that night. The agonies of his supporters caught in the train crash would not allow him.

Chapter Thirteen

A day after the train mishap, while Jamimi was still befuddled with shock, Merima and Boyama the primehead in close succession appeared on national television looking sorrowful and full of empathy for victims of the crash. Merima looking like the Good Samaritan he had been called by Chuwa radio, after condoling with families of those who died in the crash, said he was only grateful to be of help when it mattered most to the surviving victims of the crash.

Boyama in his condolence speech to the families of the victims of the crash said certain people who were supposed to be in the crashed train had been found to have *fortunately* not been in it. But he wondered where such people were and why they hadn't come out to condole with those whose relations were unfortunately in the ill-fated train.

Boyama's statement shook Jamimi out of his state of shock. 'At this moment of national grief, we must put politics behind us and give victims of the crash and their families the sympathy they deserve,' he said in a paid advert. 'To play politics with a loss like this shows lack of human feelings. Only those used to passing human beings through misfortunes or nightmares like the one caused by the train crash are capable of such lack of feelings. While some of us are still in shock, those who are not shocked by this chilling disaster rushed to radio and television houses to pay condolences that sound mocking. Shock apart, we do not have the same access to television and radio. I have to pay for my condolence. Others do not have to pay to mock the people in television and radio houses built with the people's money.

'A great tragedy has befallen our dear nation. The train crash that claimed more than a hundred lives is a claw in our hearts at this moment of national grief and for a long time to come. Our nation still in a state of shock keeps asking God why? But has God a hand in this national misfortune? After our first sin of living with evil, we should be wary of sinning against God by associating him with a wickedness harbored by the heart of man and hatched by his hand. It was not God that derailed the train but the devil. A mischief cut the rail line in Okunno forest which caused the train to crash. A mischief dug ditches in the forest and poured petrol into them to ignite the crashed train. The question is who is this mischief? This mischief must be the people who stand to benefit from the death of PLM supporters. Today, evil has developed wings soaring over our skies. If good must bring it down, it must leave the ground where it is and be a storm in the sky where evil has now taken abode and battle it to the ground. The people seeing me on television and me telling the people I am still alive wouldn't have been necessary. But we are living in times of great mischief where the wily are laying siege on the unwary to deceive them by tricks to vote for them when they hadn't retired by value the last vote that was given to them. No, I should say the last votes they stole. If the good people of this great country don't see me and I don't tell them I am still alive, on election day - a week from now, the electorates would be told I am dead and the PLM has no primehead candidate. So, UAC should be returned to power to continue doing what it knows best: living on the people instead of for the people; sapping the people instead of serving them. Members of Bivan's house, I am still alive and I am still the primehead candidate of the PLM. On May 30th, come out en masse and vote for PLM.

We are committed to attending to your present needs and allaying your fears for the future. Sharing the same heartbeat with you, we share your fears and live your dreams with you. Stand by us on election day, for as you know, whenever you look back you will see us behind you as your ever attending servants. We shall live to see the back of those currently oppressing us!'

A day after Jamimi's paid advert, Merima was on television saying it must excite national curiosity why certain people were only not in the train on the day it was to crash. Now such people had rushed to the radio and television to tell the world they were not in the train when it crashed and roasted their innocent supporters to death like grasshoppers in a wild forest fire. Such people to him sounded as if they were too happy to be alive even though those they aspire to lead were dead.

'Among normal, sane people, gain motivates mischief while loss forbids it,' Jamimi responded to Merima's speech. 'What is the gain of PLM in the death of its supporters? How can the man stalked by sharks in a boat be the one to capsize the boat? What is his benefit? What of the sharks? They have every reason to torpedo the boat into the deadly seas. People play politics to cover the tracks of their failure. The nation is dying a slow, painful death and we are here dancing to the beautiful gaze of the moon. I consider all these talk a red herring. We seem to be barking and biting very well. Let's send our dogs after the bandicoot rats stealing our groundnut instead of running our tongues over stones on which our saliva can confer no benefit. Let's face what is eating our people: The roads are bad; only the wealthy can eat two times a day; there is no water; there is no light; every social infrastructure that was healthy before UAC took over the reins of power is now sick, limping and wobbling into the grave. Let's debate on how to move our nation forward instead of snapping our fingers at each other. Let's talk on how our actions can make our people dream again.'

No one expected UAC would accept the challenge for a national debate. But it did. So it turned out that the national debate the primehead candidates of the two major political parties wouldn't have had on economic and social problems afflicting the country, the train crash forced them to. After the debate someone said to a friend, 'so anytime we want a debate on what politicians have for us, we have to cause a train to crash. Pray we will always find a train to crash.'

'That's how things are in this country particularly in the railway industry. You know employees of the railway corporation have to go on strike before they are paid any salary.'

'Government does not act to avoid disaster here but to appease one that has already occurred. Here medicine is always brought after death and it is poured as libation for the dead.'

'Everything is different here. A primehead appointed more than three hundred advisers. When asked by a visiting president from another country what he needed three hundred advisers for, he said the visiting president would not understand how things work here. The advisers were not advising him. He was the one advising the advisers.'

'Some advisers don't even have offices. Those fortunate to have offices have no desk. Those having desks have no schedule of duty.'

'Which schedule of duty are you talking about beyond gathering gossips and rumors for the primehead who is some sort of village chief? When decent folks apply themselves to earning a living by the sweat of their brows, most of these so-called advisers go about town eavesdropping on anything said about the primehead. Each adviser has a gossip or rumor deposit target the way bank employees have cash deposit targets.'

The debate between Jamimi and Merima took place three days to the election. It was the first time there was a debate by primehead candidates in Bivan's house politics. The debate was anchored by the Managing Director of Visual Communications Network.

'The taps are no longer running. What will you do about water supply if elected into office as primehead?' the Managing Director first asked Jamimi.

'It is quite embarrassing that in this century, we are still talking of how to provide clean, portable drinking water to our people when all over the world this social amenity is taken for granted. In the same way the legitimacy of any government depends on its ability to maintain law and order, it depends on its ability to provide clean portable water to the people. Most diseases are waterborne. Therefore, the cleaner the water you give your people, the healthier they are likely to be; the healthier they are, the wealthier they are. If elected as primehead, my government will spare no effort in ensuring this basic social amenity is provided for both urban and rural dwellers of our great country.'

'There is no light. What will you do about light?'

'In our modern technological age, light is a basic infrastructure. Indeed, it is the sun and oxygen of the modern industry. Without it nothing works. The soaring unemployment in the country is to some extent because of power shortages. Unemployment breeds poverty; poverty breeds crimes; crimes breed insecurity and misery. Usually, power shortages are caused by increase in power demand. This means that a reduction in power demand should reduce power shortages if it does not completely eradicate them. In Bivan's house where industries that used to place heavy demand on power supply are all dead, one would have expected that power shortages and outages would die with the dead industries. But the opposite is the case. Boyama's UAC government seems to be saying that less power demand means less power supply - an absurd outcome.

'PLM considers provision of light and water to the people as irreducible performance minimums that confer government with legitimacy no less than the maintenance of law and order. Except the order of the cemetery, what order can there be where people are sick and hungry because of lack of water and light? Under a PLM government, the bulb will replace the lantern and candle once more. As we explore the possibilities of generating power from gas and solar energy, the old, decayed turbines and transformers of our hydroelectric power generating system that cause power shortages would be replaced with new ones.

'The economy is in the woods. If elected into office how do you intend to bring it out to the plains? How will you, for example, revive textile industries that had since closed down for lack of raw materials and because they cannot compete with textiles from nations whose fabrics keep flowing into the country?'

'Lack of raw materials is artificial. We used to grow so much cotton in this country that our country was one of the major cotton exporting countries in the world. We will revive the cotton industry through mechanized farming and giving of subsidies to small cotton farmers. As for fabrics coming from outside, we will turn off the tap of free trade a little to allow for the survival of our textile industry.'

'How can you do that? Today, we are surrounded by advocates of free trade. Even here where we are, you can hear their clamor. How can you turn off the tap of free trade?'

'We can do that if we have the courage of our conviction, which we do,' Jamimi answered rapidly. 'We will freeze trade and tastes. 'We will close the sluice gates against the floods of goods coming from outside and tell our people to discipline their tastes for foreign goods. There will be protests and treachery against us, but I tell you we will not budge and we will survive and Bivan's house will prosper.'

'Under UAC your party, the whole country lies prostrate under the wind of free trade,' the director turned to Merima. 'Globalization with your party seems to mean that Bivan's house needs not produce anything because it can get all it needs from the global market. That's why even the diamonds in our country need not be polished here as we can buy polished diamonds in the global market. Is globalization only of consumption under which we are reduced only to consumers or of consumption and production under which we are required to produce something?'

'Globalization is both of production and consumption,' said Merima. 'The death of our industries didn't happen overnight. The rot started long before UAC came to power. Yes, this government has not done very well in arresting the rot and turning things around. But I assure you under me things will be different. The comatose industries would breathe again.'

'That was what Boyama said when he was campaigning to be elected.'

'Boyama is Boyama and Merima is Merima. Every tortoise carries its shell.'

'Under globalization of consumption promoted by UAC your party, members of Bivan's house have been reduced to eating, farting and defecating. We are either *eating* a car produced in Japan, a cell phone produced in Finland or a computer produced in America. How will you relocate us to thinking, production and wealth, if elected primehead?'

'Eating, farting and defecating ... Hmmm... Well, you know it is not easy getting people to leave *bonga* - a place of eating and drinking, for *malo* - a place of labor. But if elected primehead, I will relocate our people from *Bonga* to *Malo* by pointing at *Meya* - the home of want which receives those *Bonga* has pushed out.'

'Merima, market economy does not mean one should sell all one has the way your party is selling off all state-owned industries. If we go on at the rate we are going, we will soon be out of the market for want of what to sell or the money to buy it.'

'Well, you know the whole world is sieged by one view: It's either the market and democracy or under-development and poverty. We are sieged by a kind of heaven or hell bifurcation. Under this siege, if elected primehead, I will not capitulate the way Boyama seemed to have. I will check the sale of public enterprises that Boyama's government has allowed to run amok.'

'We are in the tropics. But the economy under UAC is either in winter or autumn. It is either freezing or falling like leaves from welon trees during autumn. Our economy has never known spring or summer under UAC. We suffer the burden of the temperate regions without the benefits, why?'

'I find your analogy of the economy with the weather very apt,' said Merima. 'Like the weather, the economy is a capricious thing. We can make our forecast, but the economy and the weather will determine their climate.'

During important football tournaments, football fans in Bivan's house sat round television sets to watch the matches. Shouts of excitement and clapping of hands always followed brilliant soccer displays or the scoring of a goal by fans of the side that displayed sublime soccer artistry or that scored.

It was not the same thing with the primehead television debate. Most party supporters could not understand the issues raised in the debate and so did not even bother to watch it. In the end, the debate was watched by a few enlightened members of Bivan's house who often do not go to the polling unit to vote because of the chaos and violence that usually took place at the polling units

Chapter Fourteen

'You weren't very charitable to me in that debate,' Boyama said while he and Merima were standing on the balcony of Sheraton hotel Chuwa overlooking a swimming pool. Whenever my performance was brought up, you behaved as if I am a leper you must keep at bay.'

'Would you rather I be fair to you on television and you be a fair game to Jamimi when he wins the election?'

You know I won't prefer that, but...'

'Please, understand my position. I am seeking election. I must tell the people what they want to hear. You have finished your tenure. You need no one's vote. What of me?'

'Merima is right,' said the party chairman. 'If a member of an armed robbery gang gives his fellow a tip to come and rob his office or his father, he must be thoroughly beaten like everyone else by the armed robbers to ward off suspicion of collusion with the armed robbers.'

'Are you insinuating we are armed robbers?'

'I am not insinuating anything. I am only making an analogy I think apt.'

Below a woman in a swimming trunk stood up from the pool-bed she had been lying and walked leisurely towards the swimming pool. Not far from her, another woman in a long robe, a big belt around her waist and a scarf that covered her ears was carrying what looked like a Bible in her right hand and was walking towards the gate of the hotel.

'Look at that,' said the chairman, pointing at the woman walking towards the swimming pool. 'Her buttocks have lives of their own.'

'No, look at the woman going towards the gate,' said Boyama. 'At your age, those are the kind of women you should be looking at.'

The chairman looked at the woman carrying the Bible, but quickly looked away. 'That one belongs to the holy order of the fervent sisters,' he said a wide grin on his face. 'Among the fervent sisters, the bigger the belt, the bigger the faith.'

'Which church do you attend?' asked Boyama. 'I trust it must be St Moritz. There are people that refuse to grow up. I think you are one of them. Instead of growing up, you are growing down.'

As if he had not heard what Boyama said, the chairman with his eyes riveted on the lady in a swimming trunk said, 'that lady has got both the heap and the heat.'

'The hip and the hit?'

'No, the heap and the heat. Her beauty is quick and fast. She is all perfume. That's why she would have all the bees and the wasps after her. She has the guys on their toes and whistles on their lips. Looking like this, she can start a riot on the street. She is a new song and her rhyme and rhythm intoxicate me.'

'Even with termites and dust calling you home, you still appear full of the sap of life,' said Boyama.

'Her beauty is easy, gentle, careless and unorganized. These are what make her a riot. This is what makes her a siren. See how she is scattering, no dripping grace and beauty around her as she heads for the swimming pool.'

'Your desires are not suitable to our situation,' said Merima.

'Merima, you seem to have never had the chance to live,' said the chairman. 'Instead of living life like everyone else, you are studying it.'

'Childhood is play,' said Merima. 'Youth and middle age is work while old age is pain. You are in your old age and ought to be in pains; why are you in pleasure?'

'Old age is only pain if youth and middle age weren't committed to work. If youth and middle age weren't misspent, old age would be pleasure. I didn't misspend my youth and middle age. So I deserve the pleasure I am having now.'

'Your theory is not what I see in life,' Boyama said. 'What I see in life is that old age is pains. In the pains a man finds himself in old age, he loses the taste of life and esteems it less. So, he might look upon death without the terror it held for him in his youth and childhood. Whoever in his old age has pleasure, life is not fair to him.'

'Who do you think could have been responsible for the PLM train crash?' Merima asked changing the topic. Even now with election before them he knew neither the chairman nor Boyama would be in a haste to change the topic to the challenge before them.

Though Boyama appeared to speak against the chairman's obsession with women, he was in fact enjoying the topic because like the chairman, he was enamored of women. Merima suspected

Boyama was talking about women the way he was to bait the chairman into talking more about their common obsession. As a student, Boyama once complained that when he was taught something in class, it hardly stuck to his brain. But when something was said in front of Mimi the female hostel, it stuck. One day he was on a motorcycle when thoughts about a girl he had met at a party seized his mind making him go off the road. When he regained his mind and tried to bring the motorcycle back on the road, the thought again seized him and he collided with a tree and broke his arm. Walking with his girlfriend one evening, he saw another girl and was so enchanted by this other girl that he collided with an electric pole. He always said that whenever he was in the midst of only men, he would be gasping for breath. Merima suspected Boyama first went to stand over the balcony hoping for the kind of sight they just beheld.

'I have been wondering myself,' Boyama said his mind half with Merima and half with the woman now under water. 'But, may be PLM had sworn by the rail not to do certain things they are now doing and the rail has decided to punish them,' he said going into the hotel room to ease himself. In the room he met Makwu who had just come in. A noticeable frown appeared on his face as he shook hands with Makwu and proceeded to the small room.

'It couldn't be anyone in our party that derailed that train?' Merima wondered aloud.

'As far as I know it is no one in our party,' said the chairman. 'But you know there are crackbrains in this our party. Someone incensed by the deafening popularity of Jamimi can be moved by spite to do something crazy.'

'It's big political capital to do great things in any position of authority one finds himself,' said Makwu who had joined Merima and the chairman on the balcony. 'A mere labor leader heaping up this kind of popularity because of the credible leadership he gave workers is such a big advice no one needs more.'

'With the little money he had as labor leader, he bought fertilizer for peasants,' said Merima.

'He influenced the establishment of a foundation for orphans and widows,' said Makwu

'He is a man without a price. Even the corrupt government of Hamman could not buy him,' said the chairman.

'Once in a while a name buys what money cannot,' said Merima. 'Jamimi is a guest of political fortunes because of what he did with little means he found himself in possession of. He is not only the guest of political fortunes, but the bride of political fortunes.'

'He has certainly made things trickier for us,' said a ceremonial feast who had just joined them on the balcony. 'Sometimes I wonder if we will be able to rig the forthcoming elections. If we are pushed out of power, that's that. Power in Bivan's house is so fat in returns and thin on sweat that sweat always break upon my face whenever I imagine life outside it. 'Power here is so quick in profit and slow in loss that I will be lost out of it.'

'Jamimi has vowed to change all these,' said an archer who was also on the balcony but had not spoken till then. 'He said he will make power thin on returns and fat on sweat. Our come down in the world, our descent into the gutter seems to be here.'

'Are you telling me?' said the chairman. 'Right now my chieftaincy title in my village is on the line. My story is that of Budu the palm-wine tapper. Once upon a time so went the story my father told me; Budu a palm-wine tapper was on top of a palm tree tapping the intoxicating liquid of his trade when the chief of his village - a drunken sot, took his seat under the palm tree saying, "oh you Budu the palmwine tapper. Your chief is beneath with the ants waiting to cheer his inner man." A keg of palmwine came down the tree to the chief beneath. As the sweet liquor found its way along well-beaten tracks in the chief's throat, it was hailed at different points by liquor thirsty spirits in the jag. As the spirits trumpeted the arrival of another tonic, the god of palmwine born to give pleasure to mankind whispered to the chief and he declared: "I hereby confer on you the chieftaincy title of *Eweba - the eagle on the iroko tree*, and here it comes to meet you with the empty keg of palmwine." He dropped an anklet into the empty keg, which soon ascended to Budu on the palm tree. Another keg of palmwine came down and it was welcomed with the title of *Ameyola - the one who would be chief of all palmwine tappers in the world*. Soon a violent storm swept through the forest tossing the palm tree in all dircctions. Budu on top the palm tree cried, "help! help! *Eweba, Ameyola* is falling." The treacherous drink-sodden chief shouted in reply: "throw down those titles to me; throw them down! You climbed that terrible tree to involve yourself in that horrible business without them; you will come down from it, whichever way you choose, without them."

'That chief is a palm wine oracle chief,' said the ceremonial feast. 'But jokes apart, like Budu and perhaps yourself, I may soon be getting a palmwine desertion from my harem of wives the way things are going. On top of a palm tree, the tempest of this man's chances has flung me so low. From the sybaritic grandeur of a sultan's harem, I am being flung to the depths of a man in dread of desertion. No traffic in privileges, no trading in favors of whatever kind. I am cooked, if ever any man was.'

'Knowing Jamimi the way I do, I believe, like Achimo, he will jam and jail all of us if he finds himself in that place,' panted the chairman.

'I have been told that's not his plan,' said Merima trying to scare them to more effort he would be the beneficiary of. 'His plan is to confiscate all you have and leave you wandering on the streets a frustrated and hungry man until you are run over by a vehicle. Unlike Achimo, he would not take you to prison where you will be housed and fed with public funds; more importantly, where no one will see your sunk condition and laugh at you.'

'I have always said that man does not have a good heart,' said the ceremonial feast thoroughly scared. 'How can a man nurse such an evil design against his fellow men?'

'May I die a stranger to a heart that can harbor such design,' said the chairman. 'What!'

'I can tell you we are overestimating the political consequence of this man,' said Boyama, coming back into the balcony. 'With all the rows and mows, with all the buzz and fuss about him, I tell you Jamimi is politically inconsequential. He is politically inconsequential because he is politically naïve, a bit wet behind the ear and a bit thick in the head.'

'There is something in what you are saying,' said the chairman, a new sense of wellbeing enveloping him 'Sentiments, petty gossips, small mindedness are the small ants, the little lice in his heart eating away his life, leaving behind wastes and decay. Political leeches, ticks and bedbugs around him are drawing too heavily on his goodwill and it is getting exhausted. Life is exhausted because people are drawing on it every day without replenishing it with new stock.'

'To succeed in politics, you need four things: money, myth, management and genius,' said Boyama. 'Jamimi has no money and no genius. He is badly managed. He has myth, but the myth he has is daily being exploded by poor management.'

'Merima may not have myth, but he has the genius of plotting electoral success and he enjoys good management,' said the chairman. 'Twenty years ago, Lankan had no myth, no money, but he had genius and management and he won election as primehead.'

'Well, part of what His Excellency and the chairman have said is true,' said Merima. 'But I think even for our own good, we should begin to move politics more towards service than personal aggrandizement. Politics is not about you. It's about people who need your service.'

'And you think I don't need some service from power?' asked the chairman in a high-pitched voice. 'Even though you have brought some credibility to our party, sometimes I wonder if it is such a smart thing having you on our ticket. We don't seem any safer with you than with Jamimi. It looks like whoever wins this election, we are bound for a rough deal. I moved for conquest, but people like Makwu rooted for consent. We must have a candidate we can sell to the people, as if the people count that much; as if the people have the *money* to buy anything we are selling. This is the result. We wanted salvos. We now have salvos.'

'If we are so unsure about how Merima will treat us, should we back Jamimi?' asked the ceremonial feast.

'It seems Jamimi's recent homily in Wandugu resonated with you,' said the chairman.

'What did Jamimi say in Wandugu?' asked Boyama a new look of interest on his face.

'He said something to this effect: Do not seek to prime anyone to succeed you. That is seeking to hang on when you should let go. Seeking to hang on means you still want to be in control, rule by proxy. Most people are ambitious and intelligent. They also want their hands on the levers of power. That may be even why they decided to play along with you. Once on the seat of power, like children on a swing, they will not like to sit with their hands folded on their laps, but on the chain.

They will push off your hand from the chain so as to have all the thrills of the swing that holding the chain gives. Nothing is more grieving and hurting than someone you put in power turning his back on you. You are a lot happier when you allow a free contest. Whoever wins will be full of respect for you and that's what you need and can have while out of office. Power, forget it. It is all gone when you are out of office. All you can depend on out of office is influence and influence depends on respect. Always let go when you should. Standing on is not the same thing as hanging on. Standing on you risk no fall. Hanging on you can be thrown off any moment by the speeding train. When you step out standing on, you step out with dignity. When you are thrown off while hanging on, you fall with all the indignities of being thrown off. With what dignity does a banana peel thrown away fall on the road?

But why do people want to hang to power? Greed, misuse of power. One thing leads to another. Greed for wealth makes people misuse power. One thing leads to another. When you misuse power, you are forced to want to hang on to cover your tracks and perhaps continue to misuse power. You pick a successor - someone you so much despised, to sit over your mess and cover your tracks for you. You put someone you think is a skunk and so will live with the stench of your fart and will not turn up his nose. But a skunk is known to be a traitor. Once he seizes the reins of power, he would tell you he is not your robot and it would hurt you so badly. When in power, live by the simple rules of power: do the right thing and no fear of the known or the unknown will besiege you into wanting to hang on when your time is done.

People elect you. You betray their trust and misuse the power they gave you to serve them. You are an ingrate. The people are bitter and resentful. Haunted by fear of what will happen to you out of power, you elect another person to succeed you. This is a second act of ingratitude, betrayal and contempt for the people. You weren't elected to elect others but to serve the people. Why did you leave what you were supposed to do and did another? The person you elected out of your betrayal, ingratitude and contempt for the people can only be treacherous, ungrateful and contemptuous of you. The offspring of a snake can only be a snake. The person you elected will become ungrateful to you and will heed not your bidding. A child of ungratefulness can only be ungrateful. You are bitter just like those you betrayed. The situation feeds on itself. If you allow the people to elect the one that will succeed you, you are grateful to the people and the people will be grateful and respectful of you.'

Boyama was surprised to hear this. A year ago, someone would have reported this homily of Jamimi to him the moment he made it. He had power then; he could make and mar the fortunes of men. Now he was almost out of power. All attention has shifted to Merima and Jamimi who were likely to succeed him. Even now that he was told the homily, it was by a fortuitous occurrence and not by a deliberate act of regard for him. He felt contempt for all around him. He could defy everyone and anyone and not leave power. He could postpone the forthcoming election. He could cancel it altogether. He could ban election in Bivan's house for as long as he lived. What would happen? The sky would not turn red. The air would not stop its movement. Yes, there would be a lot of noise from the so-called prodemocracy organizations. But they were all dishonest.

Which organization among the various prodemocracy organizations believed in democracy? Members of these organizations were all opportunists seeking cheap attention and funding from unsuspecting and unwary international organizations. If they truly believed in democracy and human rights, there were better ways to fight that war than the way they were affecting to fight it. The main thing threatening democracy in Bivan's house and even human rights was election rigging. How had the so-called prodemocracy organizations been fighting this scourge? After each election, they made incoherent noises on the pages of newspapers and television screens alleging massive election rigging to get cheap attention and tell their sponsors they were spending money on what they were given the money to, when the right thing to do to stop election rigging was to go to the electorates on the streets, in their homes in the rural areas before the election, long before there was talk of election and enlighten them on how to fight election rigging by being protectors of their votes. Election rigging was not magic or witchcraft. It happened before people's eyes, but they weren't able to stop it either because they had no sufficient interest in the matter or were cowardly. There were four main points of election rigging in Bivan's house: election materials collection centers, the polling units, collation centers, radio and television houses where election results were announced. If the so-called prodemocracy organizations had faith in their campaign, they would educate the people on how to resist election rigging in these centers well ahead of any election. With their sweat and blood they would comb the countryside to gird the loins of the people against those who would rob them of their choice before their own eyes. Damish alone did in Hatto state what all the so-called prodemocracy organizations which were beginning to compete with the churches for number and noise could not do because the two blights afflicting Bivan's house: dishonesty and nihilism afflicted the so-called prodemocracy organizations. Civil Society Organizations in Bivan's house were mere echoing caves echoing the firmly held beliefs and honestly prosecuted causes of like organizations elsewhere; they were a bunch of common blackmailers, another arm of advanced fee fraud - the enlightened or elegant arm of it. There was neither fire nor spark in them that he would fear if he decided to sit tight in office. But the U.S and Britain were of account in the matter. There would be a lot of bad press from these two countries. They might even humiliate him with an invasion and disgraceful removal from office. All the talk of the sanctity of national sovereignty might not amount to much, might not be sufficient shield if he incensed these countries to reprobation. 'I give it to Jamimi that he had said something there,' he said after a long interval of silence.

'But I think the windbag was letting out too much wind, if you ask me,' said the ceremonial feast.

'Actually, sometimes I am lost in his noise,' said the chairman.

'His noise is no doubt a bush one can be lost in,' said the ceremonial feast. 'I believe even he occasionally gets lost in his own noise. 'A lot of piss and wind, if you ask me,' continued the ceremonial feast after a momentary pause.

'Well, no one is asking you,' said Boyama, looking moody. 'Against Jamimi's advice, I have primed a successor,' he continued, his eyes on Merima. 'If my successor chooses to betray me after I have surrendered the reins of power to him, that's entirely his choice.'

'He dares not attempt such a thing,' said the chairman, raucously. 'In government, we shall form a ring of fire around him which he cannot step over without being singed. Merima, look at me,' he said, his eyes fixed on Merima. 'Do I look like someone you can leave in the dust of your car coughing and catching my breath after I have pushed you? We have a saying that *whoever collects the leper's money must cut his hair*. We cannot pay your passage to Jonka Palace only for you to start calling us lepers on reaching destination. I swear I will be the first person to shoot you. We cannot carry you on our backs laboring day and night the way we are now only for you to tell us we are only good enough to carry you into power and good enough to be disgraced. We cannot chase the hog with you only for you to turn your dogs on us when we have hunted it down. You cannot turn us over to misery after we have turned you over to wellbeing.'

'Well, knowing who I am,' said Boyama, 'Merima, I believe when I said, "if my successor chooses to betray me after I have surrendered the reins of power to him that's entirely his own choice," you didn't take me serious, or did you?'

There was a tense silence during which no one spoke. The eyes of Boyama were probing the face of Merima, demanding an answer.

Merima shook his head.

'Fine,' said Boyama. Turning to the chairman he said, 'you might be reckless enough to trust your life and future to gratitude, but I know the world more than that. I will not put my life in a basket outside where it would be pecked by vultures and go to sleep inside my room. I demand an oath in the shrine of Bubuluku the god of nemesis. For all I know and can see, Merima is not a suicide bomber. Seeing in my ruin his own, he would forbear from pursuing a course of action that will destroy him as much as me.'

That same night Merima was taken to the shrine of Bubuluku the god of nemesis and the oath of loyalty and allegiance to Boyama was administered on him.

Chapter Fifteen

Riots broke out on the streets of Bivan's house like a mid-day whirlwind without an eye. It was barely two years after Merima was elected primehead of Bivan's house as his party claimed or rigged into office as the opposition alleged. Tales of ballot box-snatching and ballot-stuffing, agents of the opposition abducted into farms and rivers, locked up in the booths of cars and shot point-blank abounded; yet there were no riots against these alleged acts of political gangsterism and brigandage or the election result they gave birth to. There were grumblings, in some cases rumblings, but there was no thunder. Jamimi had warned that the government of Boyama should not underestimate the grievances and frustration of the people with the way things were going in the country, saying that the people might claim what is theirs on the streets if it would not be given to them at the polling units. But the people did not file their grievances on the streets with all their show of support for Jamimi before and during the election. In fact most of his supporters said the matter should be left to God.

Shortly after the election, Jamimi's campaign manager in one of the states, said to him, 'it's God that gives power and in any power contest, whoever eventually gets it, got it with the sanction of God.'

'You mean God supports snatching of ballot boxes and falsification of results?' asked Jamimi, sarcastically.

'And shooting of innocent voters,' added the party leader.

'What then is the difference between God and the devil?' asked Mengo. 'With such a God the devil is out of business and I may as well worship the devil.'

'Each passing day in this country it is becoming increasingly difficult to distinguish the will of God from that of the devil,' said the party leader.

'It's only when something goes wrong in public affairs that we ascribed it to God,' said Jamimi. 'When a man returns home and finds his wife raped, he does not say it is an act of God. Neither do his sympathizers. Saying an evil thing is an act of God only shows our lack of hurt or outrage by it.'

'We have lost so much values and meaning that we can no longer tell God from the devil. We can no longer tell day from night. It is not only tragic, it is horror hugging us with spikes,' said Jamimi.

'When you stay long in a refuse dump the way we have, you are bound to lose many things,' said the party leader. 'After losing the value of honesty, we are losing the meaning of honesty. It is frightful indeed.'

'Conscience the policeman of the mind is on vacation here,' said Jamimi.

'That's if it has ever been on duty,' said the party leader.

'Our attitudes do not only misshape life, they abort it,' said Jamimi.

'But how did we wander so far away?' asked the party leader.

'One thing leads to another,' said Jamimi. 'We started with a culture of hypocrisy and we are ending up with a one of nihilism. We are a country of cynics and nihilists. A child of the devil goes to his father and is given favors only the devil can give and we say they are favors from God. Imagine!'

'There is no better way of showing our contempt for God than ascribing deeds of the devil to him,' said the party leader. 'If indeed we believe in God, we wouldn't be putting his face on deeds of the devil.'

'Rather than ascribe our loss to God,' said Mengo, 'I will say PLM lost because it was supported only by the masses. There was no support from the political middle class that gives power in any country. The masses are only a heap of sand. They need the political middle class constituted by the elites to give life to them. Without the support of the political middle class, Jamimi was left swinging and twisting in the wind without an anchor.'

Seeing the people would not file their grievances on the streets, Jamimi filed his grievances in the court. He called three hundred and six witnesses to prove election rigging, violence, intimidation and falsification of results, but the court said he should have called one hundred and fifty thousand witnesses to be able to have the election nullified.

Periodically, there were fuel scarcities in Bivan's house. Then long queues were seen at the few filling stations there was fuel - giving Bivan's house on the roadsides the trains it no longer had on the railtracks. However, whenever fuel disappeared from the filling stations, it miraculously appeared in big and small jerry cans in the black market, sold at prohibitive prices by fuel vendors on the streets. Overnight, street urchins became independent fuel marketers charging exorbitant prices for their merchandise. Those who had no time to spend at the filling stations, but had money bought their fuel from the black-market fuel vendors.

It was to the street fuel vendors that someone likened the judges of Bivan's house after an election. Each election in the country seemed to spawn injustice the way frogs spawn eggs in a pond. Candidates who had lost out at the polling units headed to the election tribunals seeking to get in the court the justice they could not get at the polls. However, often the decisions of the courts were rigged the way the election was. Overnight, judges the dispensers of justice became independent judicial marketers selling justice to the highest bidder like the fuel vendors so much that when a judge made an order of injunction against the holding of a rally to protest rigged election results, the opposition referred to the court order as *a black-market injunction.*

High court judges in Bivan's house were paid a salary no public servant was. Many people suspected that the extraordinary salary the judges were paid was an official bribe by the government to make them favor the government in any case it had an interest. After the election petition filed by Jamimi was dismissed, a supporter of the PLM walking away from the court in shock and frustration said, 'He who pays the piper dictates the tune.'

'That's the white man's saying,' said his friend walking beside him. 'In Africa the saying is *whoever greets the canoe man in the dry season will be the first to cross the river during the rainy season.* The government of Boyama was greeting the judges in the dry season and that's why it is the first to cross the river now.'

'Only that it wasn't their breath and voices they were using to greet the judges. It was our voices and breath,' someone said.

'Is it only greeting? They were shaking hands with the judges,' said another person.

'Only that it was our hands they were using to shake the judges. And they were doing so without our consent,' added somebody. Other people angry with the court's judgment went on to express their resentment.

'Despite the fat salaries the judges are paid, they still collect bribes.'

'When the heart of a man is full of holes no fat poured into it nourishes it.'

'The court that ought to be the touchstone of justice has turned into a cesspool of corruption and injustice.'

'You remember the judge who after collecting bribes from both the plaintiff and defendant in his judgment said both parties won the case before him?'

Everyone laughed. It was a case most of them had heard of.

Jamimi filed an appeal to the Supreme Court. It was while the matter was still pending in the Supreme Court that the riots broke out not on account of the unjust election or the trial court's decision that legitimized it, but for an altogether different reason.

As with the election, there was no protest against the trial court's verdict which many people said was purchased by the ruling UAC government. The matter like many others that had been left for God by the people was left for him by the people.

'I wonder when God will dispose of all these cases we have been filing in his court,' someone said when his neighbor said they should leave the outcome of the court's decision to God.

'Well,' said the neighbor, 'these cases are merely for God's information. It is never intended he should adjudicate on them, at least not in a hurry.'

'Now Boyama has succeeded in leaving his photograph called Merima in Jonka Palace.'

A photograph is not necessarily a bad thing. It is only bad when it is the picture of a bad man.'

'How can Merima be his own man given how he became primehead? To fly, he was given chains for wings by the man who said he would make him an eagle.'

'If the reason of leaving his picture behind is the fear of retribution, I think Boyama needed not have done that. His excesses in government were such that he can plead insanity if arraigned before any court. I understand insanity is a defense to a charge at law.'

'There is no doubt that lunacy is a defense Boyama can plead before any judge before whom his atrocities are testified to.'

Only that the judges he would be pleading insanity before are themselves insane. It takes a sane man to appreciate insanity.'

'Why is power poison here?'

'In life, everything is poison and nothing is poison. It depends on how much of a thing one allows into himself.'

Merima seemed so buzzed by power that when he is walking his legs hardly touch the ground again.'

'Life has become a dream with him.'

'Only that he might wake up in a nightmare.'

'Not in Bivan's house. Boyama who ought to be out of power on a limp is out with a bounce. So, it will be with Merima.'

'To think that my own name is Boyama; he has used up that name leaving us his namesakes without names.'

'That's the price you pay when you share a name with a more known person. He would use up the name and leave you without a name.'

'This price is higher when the known man is a bad man. He not only uses up the name, he infects it with leprosy.'

Where Jamimi expected the fire would start, it did not start there. Instead, it started where no one least expected. The riots started from an argument between two members of the UAC that went to the office of a ceremonial pot for handouts which were referred to as *syringe* among political panhandlers. As the hospital syringe injects blood into anaemic patients, the political *syringe* injected money into the empty pockets of political hangers-on.

There were two industries in Bivan's house that at all times were always in business: politics and religion. You could only make money either in politics or religion. There was money from diamonds which was used to import cheap goods into the country; so producing any type of goods was unprofitable. But if you were a good public speaker and could found a church, people driven by the misery of their present life and hopeful of reprieve in the hereafter would flock to your church with their tithes and thanks-giving money even when there was nothing to be thankful for, except of course thanking God that there was *heaven* beyond the present hell. So, you could found a church anywhere and under any name with reasonable expectations of patronage.

Those who were not *called* to the church or mosque were *called* to politics the other thriving industry. However, unlike religion with a wide space, the space in politics was narrow. Political offices were few. However, whoever managed to occupy one was sure of becoming rich. For those in politics who were not occupying political office, but wanted to be rich through the bonanza and patronage of those occupying political offices or seeking election into such offices, the space for achieving wealth was also narrow. Unlike in religion where the poor who were many pay tithes to the priests who were few, in politics the electorates who were many demanded *syringe* from those occupying or seeking election into public offices who were few. Worse, often only candidates contesting for political offices under UAC had *syringe* to give the electorates.

Since only UAC candidates could give *syringe* and most political office holders were UAC members, everyone flocked to that party so much that the party was likened to a *molue* - an old rickety bus, where those standing were more than those sitting. It was among those standing that the quarrel which led to the riots started.

Chokali a huge, walloping man, an accomplished political thug was the first to arrive the office of the ceremonial pot that Monday morning. For him, the world did not sleep well the previous night and it seemed to have woken up in a rage that morning. When he left his house for the office of the ceremonial pot, the world was wearing a frown on its not too pretty face and he himself affected the air that disaster was an attaché of. He ate very little the previous night because there was little to eat. He was going to the ceremonial pot's office with the hope that he would give him some money to feed himself and his family. During electioneering campaigns and election, he never went without food. He always had money to feed himself and his family and even drink beer with. That was his season. His services either as a bodyguard or a thug were needed by the politicians. So, they brought out the money. One even gave him so much money that he returned some of it to the man. But now that elections were over, no politician was ready to give him money and when he was given, it was so paltry it could scarcely feed him, lest his family. Politicians were such mean and miserly fellows that the only thought in their minds at any time was *use and dump*. He was moved to spite and contempt for them. They appeared big in their overflowing gowns, but small in their minds. On his way to the ceremonial pot's office, he was swearing to himself that he would never be the fool he was during the last election. Any politician needing his services during election had to pay dearly for it.

When he got to the ceremonial pot's office and found himself the only person waiting to see the ceremonial pot who was already in the office, there was a visible improvement in his cheer. Mondays and Fridays were days there were more people trooping to the offices of political office holders begging for handouts than any other day of the week. On Friday, they begged for handouts that would see them through the weekend. On Monday whatever they had before the weekend was exhausted during the weekend. It was therefore cheering for him to find only himself waiting to see the ceremonial pot. It meant he was likely to get something substantial from the ceremonial pot. It was in this buoyant spirit that Gurungutsi another panhandler arrived the ceremonial pot's office. The moment he saw him, his countenance which before then had been radiant turned cloudy. From the clouds on his face, rain was to later fall, not only on Gurungutsi, but on many members of Bivan's house that were not in the ceremonial pot's office.

Chapter Sixteen

'Were you not the fellow I saw in the office of the adviser on food security last Friday?' Chokali asked, his voice full of offence. Part of the reason he got so little money from the adviser on Friday was the presence of people like Gurungutsi and he was around again today to share his cut.

'I am,' Gurungutsi said, tonelessly.

'What has brought you to the ceremonial pot's office so early today?' Chokali asked.

'I should be asking you that question. I met you here,' said Gurungutsi.

'I am a member of UAC and this is a UAC office.'

'I am also a UAC member.'

'You are not. Several times I have seen you at PLM's rallies? You are a member of PLM. Why are you following offices of UAC members begging for alms? Why are you reaping where you didn't sow?'

'Yes, I was formerly a member of PLM. But that was more than a year ago. Since then, I have been a UAC member. I hold a UAC membership card.'

'You are lying. You are still a PLM member reaping where you haven't sown.'

'What have you sown in the UAC?'

'Every member of UAC knows what I have sown in my party. It is only PLM members who weren't around during the planting season, but who shamelessly turn up for the harvest that do not know what I sowed. I swear we will not allow PLM members and supporters to continue fishing in UAC waters, poaching in UAC forests. They must be shown the way out.'

'See how your mind runs - thinking only in terms of fishing and poaching. Not in terms of service. Not in terms of giving useful advice to people in government on how to serve our people well.'

'What advice are you here to give today? That the ceremonial pot should be sharing his feeding money with us?'

'No, that he should sink a borehole in my village.'

'Liar!'

'Thief!'

'You are calling me a thief?' Chokali slapped Gurungutsi and the two began to fight. The ceremonial pot came out of his office shouting at his messenger to throw out the two fighting nuisances. The messenger, who was just returning from a small canteen he ate at every morning, pushed the two fighting men out of the office. From a nearby street, Benbendo, an early morning drunk from the same village with Chokali, staggered out of a gutter, saw the two men fighting and began singing and dancing, jerking his body and shuffling his feet in a weird, uncoordinated manner:

Chokali o Chokali o
Mmmmmmmmh
O wo Chokali o
Bakan sisi kikya nang gyi kwan a
mmmmmmmmh
O wo Chokali o.

It was an old song that Chokali knew. It was a song way down his roots. It was a song he sang as a child. It was a song he hadn't heard a long time off. Hearing it now reconnected him with the innocence of his childhood and the very rhythm and heartbeat of life in the village he was born and bred. This was a song sung by drunks. The original name in the song was Joromi, not Chokali. The drunk now singing the song knew

Chokali and that was why he had replaced Joromi with Chokali. The song asked drunks that were fighting over five baduns beer why they should be fighting over a dram.

On hearing the song, Chokali pulled himself out of the fight and Gurungutsi who didn't have his heart in the fight did not hold him to it. As the drunk sang the song over and over again dancing on the street, tears came to Chokali's eyes. The drunk clearly didn't know what they were fighting over. He wasn't where the fight begun and so could not know what started it. He was only a drunk singing a song he would sing in a beer house if there was a brawl over beer or in the bliss of intoxication that he might sing without even such a fracas. But the song now was a rebuke to Chokali asking him why he should be fighting over pittance with another poor man who like him was only scavenging about for crumbs from the table of their common oppressor. Gurungutsi standing and watching him was shocked to see tears flowing freely on Chokali's cheeks. Even though he didn't know what the song was about because he didn't understand the language of the song, and even though he didn't know the relationship of Chokali with the song, he could see it was the song that was having this dramatic effect on his assailant. Moving from shock to awe, he stood watching Chokali and the drunk, his mouth agape. After a while, the drunk danced away and was lost to their sight.

Chokali walked to Gurungutsi and apologized to him for fighting a victim like himself instead of their common oppressor.

'Was that what he was telling you by his song?' Gurungutsi asked, still perplexed by the drama unfolding before him.

'It wasn't exactly what he was telling me, but what he was saying opened my eyes to see our situation in the light of what I just told you. Where I come from, we receive revelations from mad men and a drunk is a mad man. What that man had just said in the song he sang is a revelation and I will act on it. Follow me and see how I will turn things upside down in this country.' Without waiting to know whether Gurungutsi would follow him or not, Chokali removed his cap from his head, gave a whoop and started running shouting: 'The government of Boyama and the apology he left behind in Jonka Palace have stolen all the money of Bivan's house. There is no light, no water and no food because the money to provide these necessities has been stolen by government. Poor members of

Bivan's house, arise and reclaim your lives!' He ran for not more than five hundred meters; but when he looked back, he was shocked to see thousands of people behind him.

'Poverty has slapped me with its left hand!' chanted Chokali.

'The last meal of insults that poverty serves a poor man is a slap with the left hand!' chanted the rioters.

'When poverty slaps you with its left hand…'

'It gives a sword to you with its right hand for you to find dignity again.'

'Wielding the sword of poverty in our hands, we rise from the ground we fell when poverty slapped us to demand our due.'

'They think we are horses for them to ride.'

'Yes, we are horses, but they are the straw we will eat!'

Two days after the riots erupted, Jamimi sitting with the party leader, Mengo, Talgon and some party members remarked to the party leader; 'it is now clear that Bivan's house was a gigantic fuel tank waiting for a spark to burst into flames. But the tank was not marked 'Highly Inflammable' and that was perhaps why Chokali struck a match near it.'

'Even if it were marked, how do you expect a drunk and a thug to have read and made sense of the marking?' said the party leader.

'Before the eyes of a drunk, the world is dancing and when something is dancing, it is difficult to pick anything out of it,' said Mengo, wincing expansively. The bee seemed to have stung him severely.

'Because the drunk sees the world dancing, is that why he is always dancing?' asked Talgon.

'I think so,' said a party member.

'I fear that beer in the mouth of the drunk that started these riots has not entered the riots. Their ferocity alarms even me who does not wish the government well. We might all be consumed in the fury blazing through the country. You know what happened to the cockroach when he started a fire to spite the rat. Both he and the rat were consumed by that fire,' said the party leader.

'Only that we didn't start this fire, 'said a party member.

'It is now clear that what the people wanted, were waiting for all the years of perfidy and misrule by the UAC is action, not rhetoric on radio and the pages of newspapers, said the party leader.

'Everyone can now see that an ounce of action is worth more than a pound of rhetoric,' said Talgon. 'Words are brushed aside. But no one can brush action aside. It must be listened and hearkened to.'

'You know talking is like the wind of everyday life. It unsettles no one and no one heeds it. But action is a storm that spins people and brings them to their senses,' said a party member. The party members went on talking among themselves.

'Action shouts and screams at people. Talking merely whispers to them.'

'Action is thunder. Talking is the distant rumbling of the skies.'

'Talking is a lot of piss in the wind.'

'It is a lot of fart in the water.'

'Politics played on the streets by street people is now fighting on the streets.'

'The street has infected politics with madness.'

'From what I heard, Chokali the thug who started the riots was provoked into action by the song of Benbendo a drunk from his village,' said the party leader who had a way of scooping news other people could not access. 'The revolution you Jamimi the *generalissimo supremo* of oration could not trigger with all your linguistic artistry and mental sagacity, a drunk spilling obscenities on the street has whipped up. It is so uncanny. But this is Bivan's house where things are always bewildering.'

'Well, we are now put to the test and the task,' said Jamimi. 'We wanted to get to Jonka Palace in a zephyr, but it turned out it's a whirlwind that's available for the trip. So we have to ride in what has presented itself to us. There was a feast in a faraway land. The tortoise wanted to attend that feast. So did the antelope. So did many other animals. So many animals were attending the feast that before the tortoise crawled to it, the feast would have been over. The tortoise knowing the antelope would attend the feast went and tied himself to the tail of the antelope the night before the feast. When the antelope woke up and began racing to the feast, he was racing with the tortoise tied to his tail. He assumed the weight on his tail to be the weight of dew that fell the previous night. We will hang onto the tail of the antelope racing through Bivan's house now to take us to Jonka palace.'

'Now we have to offer them leadership in what we didn't start,' said a party member.

'Their resentment is feckless and unorganized; we have to organize it and concentrate it on the government where it hurts most,' said Talgon. 'Let's turn the plague of violence on the streets into a plague of thunder and hail that will chase Merima out of power. Let's turn the riot into a rebellion.'

'If they have no ambition of seizing power and reorganizing society on more egalitarian principles, we have to give them such ambition,' said Jamimi. 'Let's turn the rebellion into a revolution. Let's twist the knife the mob has stuck into the guts of this bloodsucking government and make it scream with pain. Today I will be on radio to urge the rebellion on.'

'That will be sticking our necks out and I don't think I can stick my neck out for this country today,' said the party leader. 'Yesterday, I might have done so; not today. There was once a nation worth fighting and dying for. That nation died with Achimo the great patriot of Bivan's house. The new nation means nothing to me. It does not reach me. It shares little of me and I share little of it.'

'Bivan's house may be long dead with you, but it is still a feeling with me, and it is a very strong feeling,' said Jamimi.

'Different folks, different strokes,' murmured the party leader. 'As far as I am concerned, let it be with Bivan's house according to the designs of its fate.'

'What you are saying is a prescription for death,' said Jamimi, alarmed by what the party leader said. 'If we can't help ourselves, who will help us? I think the Buddha was right when he said you should not look to anyone for salvation but yourself. Even though Jesus was supposed to have died for our sins, we still have to stay away from sin to be deserving of his salvation. The wretchedness and misery of life is that no one gives you anything. You have to earn everything by the force of your ability and drive. If you don't claim what is yours, the person who seized it from you will keep it and be mocking you while he gobbles up your due. The hyena is never known to let go a goat it has caught without a fight. Neither is the hawk known to let go a chick in its claws without howls from the owner of the chick.'

'That's an exquisite exposition of life,' said Mengo, something like a mild amusement plastered on his face. 'But you know chasing a hyena bare fisted is dangerous. Neither is it easy to chase a hawk when you have no wings. You see how perilous and daunting our enterprise can be?'

'Besides,' said the party leader, we still have our matter in the Supreme Court. Taking a position such as you recommend will pre-empt the outcome of that case.'

'I am under no illusion as to what the outcome of that case would be, but filed it simply to make our judges further ridicule their offices and to free myself from charges of being bought over by the UAC. Ten years ago, I lost confidence and faith in our judiciary. The corruption and ineptitude of the judges apart, the fraud in the last election was so monumental it can hardly be addressed by any court. There are certain degrees of unlawfulness that can't be cured by recourse to law but by recourse to a proportionate degree of unlawfulness on the streets. The last election was that kind of unlawfulness and that's why I want us to take advantage of what is happening now to redress it. Tonight, we will light up the riots with the incandescence of a national struggle for the emancipation of the people from the shackles of poverty and deprivation which nature by her generosity of endowments has insulated them from, but which their government by its corruption and incompetence has exposed them to. Those yet to come out must come out and join those on the streets struggling to secure a better future for themselves and their children. The struggle is no longer a book and pen struggle, but a gun and canon struggle. What is needed to seize the reins of power in Jonka Palace is street power, not the rhetoric of books and the pen. That's why I will join them on the streets. '

'It's not only your neck you would be putting into the noose by joining the rioters on the street, but our necks as well and neither of us is ready for such a stiff price,' Mengo said, looking grave. 'I have children and a wife who have a stake in my life and they have told me not to toy with their wellbeing by toying with my life.'

'As for me,' said the party leader, 'my life is yet to lose all the meaning and tensions that preserve it for me to want to throw it away and Jamimi I will not support you throwing yours away either.'

'I used to think you are a fetish of power,' said Talgon.

'And so I am. But not to the point of losing my life in the chase of it. I am a long-haired wise man, not a long-haired fool.'

'As a fetish of power, the leader can see disaster coming which you can't,' said Mengo.

'This is our problem in this country,' Jamimi said in a very sad tone. 'Everyone is holding onto life even as life like an eel is slipping away from him. There is the picture of this poor woman and her child that I will never forget. The bus she was travelling in with her child had a fatal accident in which many people died. The poor woman and her child survived. Clutching her child with one hand to her wizened chest, the poor woman with her knees on the ground amidst the wreckage of the accident raised the other hand to God in thankfulness to him for sparing her life. I asked, sparing her life for what? Thinking she was living she forgot she was dead. That was the sad situation in Bivan's house a few days ago. We would rather live on our knees than die with dignity on our feet. But I am happy that this is no longer the situation in the country. The poor, at least most of them, have discovered that death is a creeping certainty. It's either they die on the streets fighting for their rights or of hunger in their homes. They have chosen to die on the streets fighting for their rights and I am joining them. It is sad you are behind the times. Your thoughts are not contemporary thoughts but thoughts of bygone times. How can you be thinking of what to eat on a day that is not yours? Today is your day and you have something to eat. The best thing you can do for tomorrow is to fight for what you will eat tomorrow if you live to see it and that's what our people are doing on the streets. Whoever is not thinking like the men and women on the streets, his head is not screwed on the right side of his neck and on the right side of history.'

'I will rather have my head screwed on the wrong side of my neck than have a noose slipped over it,' said the party leader.

'I am with you where you are,' said Mengo, wincing and massaging his jowl. 'It is always wiser to outlive the oppressor by cowardice than by bravery give him the joy of sneering at your grave. Besides, there is already madness in the land. It will do for us what we want done without us risking our own heads.

'We have to stoke the fire or it will flare out and that's what I will not allow to happen,' said Jamimi. 'The mad man dancing on the street can't be dancing and beating the drum all by himself. For him to continue dancing, we have to beat the drum for him, and that's what I will do.'

Chapter Seventeen

The riots degenerated into street urchins collecting, on threat of violence, what they called *wayward money*. Overnight *wayward money* became tolls motorists and even pedestrians had to pay to street urchins and gang boys before they were allowed to move beyond the point the street urchins or gangs were. The roads were now under siege and one could only venture out of doors if he had money to settle the demons of the streets. Whoever was on the street and could not pay his way through because he had no money was stripped of his clothes and his back was branded with a knife or razor blade NO MONEY. The street urchins would then tell him that what he now carried on his back was the mark of Satan and it would henceforth be his pass on the streets.

The urchins' tollgates were random, spontaneous and wild. Without the least warning or foreboding, a motorist or pedestrian could find himself surrounded by street urchins demanding a fee from him before he could move beyond the point he was. If he could not pay, he was given the mark of Satan and pushed off into the world to spread the new gospel in Bivan's house.

Jamimi coming from his regular exercise in a nearby gymnasium ran into an army of street urchins who demanded from him *wayward money.*

'*Wayward money*?' Jamimi who had heard of the wayward ransom, but had never had to pay it asked a little astounded by the brashness and seediness of the youths that had surrounded him.

'Yes, *wayward money* or your ancestors will receive you the way they won't want to.'

'What does *wayward money* mean?'

'It is a tax everyone now has to pay for the maintenance of wayward people.'

'And who are these wayward people?'

'We are. We live on the street and so we are wayward.'

'Everyone in Bivan's house is wayward. The country is a wayward country. In a way the wayward levy is for everyone.'

'Why do you levy this tax?'

'We levy this tax because we don't benefit from the wealth of this country. We have set up our own government on the streets. The tax is for our government. This is a wayward country where everyone does what he likes. We are doing what we like, like everyone else.'

'Everyone is doing what he likes? That's terrible.'

'Yes, everyone does what he likes. Archers in the house of archery have fixed fabulous and fantastic salaries and allowances for themselves. Big feasts fixed disengagement allowances for themselves that terminate their governance in a pool of money and they are laughing in both their mouths and ears. Yes, everyone may do as he likes.'

'It is obscene to demand money the way you are doing.'

'We are living in a country that is an obscene mass of concentrated sins.'

'People in government are settled in their offices. What is not obscene about that? We have no office, but we have the streets and that is where we have to be settled. Armed robbers are settled on the highways far off the towns. What is not obscene about that? We have no fire arms, but we have knives and the streets; on the streets we must be settled. The police are licensed to set up roadblocks to collect tolls, we have no license but we hold the terror of the streets and we shall wield it to collect our tolls. Your toll, or the mark of Satan on your back!'

'We have drawn up a new charter for society on the street. In our charter the *wayward levy* is a legitimate tax.'

'Throughout history those who make laws make laws approving what is good for them and prohibiting what is bad for them. We have not done anything strange or unconventional.'

'Those making laws are sieged by their interest to make only laws favorable to themselves.'

'The law against stealing is by the rich who benefits from it not the poor who are its victims.'

'Whenever you see a poor man applauding the law prohibiting stealing, he has been manipulated by the rich to spite himself.'

'We of the street are smart and clever people. No one can manipulate us to hate ourselves.'

'Throughout history no one has been his brother's keeper and we are not pretending to be our brothers' keepers. Everyone for himself. God for us all.'

'Nothing is good for everyone and nothing is bad for everyone. Rain is good for plants but bad for the maize spread outside to dry. Fire is good for the person using it to cook his meal, but bad for the wood burning; the cat is the consort of the house owner, but the nightmare of the rat.'

'Our parents were deceived to believe in order. But we have found that order serves only the interest of a few parasites. We have drawn up a charter of disorder. Let's see who it will serve.'

'How much is the fee I must pay?' Jamimi asked now desperate to get away from the urchins. He has just observed that more urchins were pouring into where they were and these urchins looked wilder than the ones that first stopped him.

'Five thousand baduns'

'Have it, but please leave the streets.'

'We have sowed our hearts on the streets.'

Before his encounter with the urchins on the street, Jamimi had been of the mind of leading the protests on the streets against the government of Merima. His encounter with the urchins decided him firmly on this course. From what he could see the country had sunk into lawlessness. Unless the government of Merima was brought to an end quickly, there would be no country for him or anyone to aspire to govern. So, he must lead the protests to abort the total failure of Bivan's house project.

Both the PLM leader and Mengo put so much pressure on Jamimi not to lead the protests that in the end he agreed to do as they would have him. But it was a ruse to throw off the pressure they were piling on him. The following day, he was seen in front of a group of rioters wielding a machete and chanting that the government of Merima and Boyama must go. His new political party was the mob on the street, not PLM besieged by thoughts of self-preservation.

Chapter Eighteen

'Both Boyama and Merima are a plague on this country,' chanted Jamimi in front of the rioting mob he was leading. 'They are a league of leeches sucking our live blood and making us anaemic. Both Merima and Boyama are standing on their last legs. We should pull down the legs that keep them standing on us. Both Boyama and Merima are secretariats of greed and the people have risen up to demolish those secretariats. Like sharks they ought to push their stomachs out and wash them clean or else they would burst of the lucre they had swallowed. One thing leads to another. Stupidity breeds greed. Greed breeds corruption. Corruption breeds sieges, barricades and pickets that create fears of losing power. We are on the streets as the nemesis of those who swallowed what they should have shared with others. One thing leads to another! Their original sin is stupidity, which has infected them with incurable greed! All intelligent people know it is stupid to put up wealth for a day that is not yours. Because all intelligent people know that wealth is matter that will be eaten by moths and termites with the passage of time, they do not invest their future in it. It is stupid people that know and think otherwise. All intelligent people know it is wise to invest in a name because a name is air that neither moths nor termites can eat. It is stupid people that know and think otherwise. The people have risen up to claim their dignity and destiny from those who are feeding termites and moths with their dignity and destiny. There is going to be an exchange program very soon. The people will have their dignity and destiny back. But moths and termites need not worry much. They will be fed with the flesh of those who have been feeding them with the dignity and destiny of the people.'

Unknown to Jamimi and the rioting mob, at the time they were walking the streets of Bivan's house calling for the heads of Boyama and Merima the primehead, Boyama and Merima had no heads. It was in the early hours of the night that news of the primehead and Boyama's death broke out in the media. Boyama was reported to have been killed by a mob of rioters that broke into his residence at Nopak while the primehead was shot dead in Jonka jungle by unknown assassins. After he was sworn in as primehead, Merima's hunting habits and going into the forest alone seemed to intensify to the chagrin of his wife and government officials whose prestige and livelihood were tied to his being the primehead. It was not only in the day time that he went hunting in the jungle of Jonka Palace, but even in the night. His wife had complained and cried against this recklessness of her husband to no avail. Seeing him as a disaster waiting to happen, she resigned herself to fate. The People who did not know the primehead's hunting habits were shocked more by how and where the primehead died than by the fact of his death. The two men were reported to have been killed at close intervals - Boyama first. But it was not clear whether Merima knew of Boyama's death before his own death or he did not know.

The primehead and the deputy primehead even before the election were not political soul mates. They were joined on the primehead ticket out of political necessity not because they were compatible or of the same political sway. While Merima was quiet and unassuming, the deputy primehead has always behaved like a man whose destiny needed to move fast to catch up with him. He was overbearing not only to his inferiors, but sometimes even to the primehead. In power circles, he was seen as a megalomaniac. Now that the primehead had been shot dead and it was not known who did it, suspicion was on the deputy primehead. By the constitution of Bivan's house, now that the primehead was dead, he was to be sworn in as primehead.

'But not if he had a hand in the death of the primehead,' said the party chairman in an emergency meeting called to deliberate on the death of the primehead and succession to his office. Because succession was to be discussed in the meeting and the deputy primehead was by constitutional provisions the automatic successor, he was excused from the meeting. The chairman has never hidden his dislike for the deputy primehead and he was not hiding it now. With Merima, he had a big voice in government because power was not such an obsession with Merima. But with a megalomaniac like the deputy primehead, he was sure to want to hold all the levers of power in his hand and this held a morbid scare for the chairman.

'What!' cried a crony of the deputy primehead, jumping up from his seat and making to go over to where the chairman of the party was sitting, but he was held back by those sitting near him.

'What we need in this meeting is restraint,' said the party secretary. 'We have just suffered violence; more violence will not help us.'

'When something like this happens, people are bound to have their suspicions. There is no harm in nursing such suspicion in our hearts so long as they are not expressed,' said an elder of the party invited to the meeting. 'But if they are expressed, more terrible things than what happened might happen.'

'I owe no one apology for what I said, particularly those who hope the deputy primehead might favor them with the largesse of office if he becomes primehead,' said the chairman, looking straight at the crony of the deputy primehead. 'To prove that I owe no one apology for what I said, I repeat that the deputy primehead can't be sworn in as primehead if it is proved that he had a hand in the primehead's death. Killing the primehead is treason under our constitution punishable with death. Whoever therefore killed the primehead can't be primehead.'

There was complete silence now in the primehead's chambers where the meeting was holding. The deputy primehead's crony who had reacted violently to the first declaration of the chairman showed no sign of protest again when the chairman repeated what he had said. He had cautioned himself to take it easy. Much as he was closed to the deputy primehead, he could not be too sure of the deputy primehead favoring him with a fat appointment if he becomes primehead. The deputy primehead was a very treacherous and deceitful politician. He could betray anyone at any time if in his cold political calculations that would serve his ends better. When the chairman said, 'those who hope the deputy primehead might favor them with the largesse of office if he becomes primehead,' he was perhaps alluding to the treacherous character of the deputy primehead. It seemed other people at the meeting sympathetic to the deputy primehead like the crony who impetuously reacted to the chairman's insinuations were now thinking the same way the crony was; for they too did not challenge the chairman when he repeated what he first said.

'The primehead was shot dead in Jonka Palace jungle and no one knows who did it,' said the secretary of the party. 'It's natural to suspect the deputy primehead who has access to Jonka palace and who stands to benefit from the death of the primehead.'

'But there is a riot against the government of Merima in the country which has claimed the life of Boyama and many other high-profile politicians. One of the rioters could have shot the primehead,' said the deputy primehead's crony. He must not totally abandon the deputy primehead to the dislike of the chairman and his supporters. More than anyone in that meeting, the deputy primehead counted on him to protect his interest. If he did not and eventually the deputy primehead gets the office, someone is sure to gossip to him that his man after all did not stand up for him when it mattered most. Even the chairman for all his hatred of the deputy primehead could pass such a gossip to the deputy primehead for a favor if he becomes primehead. Even if he did not become primehead, someone might yet tell him how he was betrayed by those he relied on, only in this case he had little to worry over because the deputy primehead without power was of no use to him. In fact if he was charged and convicted for the murder of the primehead, he would be of no use to himself, least another person.

'You know as well as we do that what you are saying is not possible,' said the chairman. 'How could such a rioter gain access into Jonka palace's jungle? We all know how fortified it is.'

'The primehead could have killed himself,' said the crony, impulsively. 'Boyama died before him. If he heard of Boyama's death as I am sure he did, he could have become so distracted and disoriented as to kill himself. Boyama was the pillar on which he hung. If the pillar holding the roof gives way, the roof might give way as well.'

What the crony said struck a chord with some people. Merima was never meant for the kitchen of politics with all its heat and smoke. In the kitchen, he was always talking of life being a siege and that was why he went hunting to escape from the siege. With all the riots, he must have felt the siege so acutely that the forest might no longer be affording him an escape. Hearing of the death of his political prop could make him kill himself to escape permanently from the siege.

'Kolaha, I learned you were born in a village without a nearby river or stream,' said the chairman, addressing the deputy primehead's crony. 'People in your village go very far to fetch their drinking water. This water you have fetched from the far away stream of your village, no one will drink it with you. Whoever killed the primehead wants us to think the way you want us to think, but you can bet your life on it that I will not think that way.'

'Where in the whole wide world has any primehead ever committed suicide?' asked the organizing secretary. 'Who will snuff out his life, leaving all the perks and perquisites of such an office?'

'Unless, if he was insane?' said the deputy primehead's crony.

'Are you insinuating Merima was insane? We should be wary of what we say particularly against a man who can no longer defend himself,' said the organizing secretary.

'I am not saying anything against him. I am only saying we should avert our minds to all possibilities. We should not close the door against any thought.'

'Well, the primehead wasn't insane and we all know it. So that door you were opening is closed,' said the chairman.

'Not so fast,' said the deputy primehead's crony. 'Madness need not be a long-drawn thing that everyone must know. It can be a brief spell that no one knows nothing of. It could have just descended upon him in the forest while he was hunting. There are forest spirits that bring sudden madness upon people.'

'Kolaha, you are even stretching your reasoning too far. Is it normal for a primehead to go hunting alone in the forest? Is it even normal for him to go hunting at all? When God created the world, he dropped logic into it and it has been what has been holding the world together. We must be courageous enough to say with our mouths what we are thinking in our heads,' said the legal adviser of the party who had some sympathy for the deputy primehead.

'Yes, it might be abnormal for the primehead to go into a forest, but it is not abnormal for a man to have a hobby,' said the chairman. 'Hunting has been the primehead's hobby right from childhood and he had indulged himself in that fancy without anyone saying he was mad and without him taking his own life.'

'No one might have raised flak against the primehead's hobby before he became primehead,' said the legal adviser. 'But when he became primehead, the situation changed. His life was no longer his, but that of members of Bivan's house. They are entitled to question a hobby that undermines the dignity of the office of primehead which by the way is the sum total of the dignity of Bivan's house members. For me, the primehead might not be mad, but we should not be in a haste to overlook suicide in the circumstances of the primehead's death.'

'Bizarre things are happening in this country today,' said Kolaha. 'If no one is seeing them, I am. Before now it was unthinkable that ordinary members of Bivan's house would rise up against the central might the way they had done now. It was suicide to do so. If ordinary members of Bivan's house who could not commit suicide before are now doing so, why not their primehead?'

'It is sad that the police were too quick to kill the drunken man that started this orgy of violence. I believe there is more to this thing than what we know and are seeing,' said the legal adviser. 'If the drunk who started the madness were alive, we would have quizzed him and perhaps get to the bottom of it. But he is dead leaving behind his spirit to fan the fire he ignited.'

'Even Chokali the thug the drunk pushed to start this bloodletting has been killed. If he were alive, he would have told us what exactly entered his head when the drunk started singing,' said the organizing secretary. For a while the meeting dissolved into a talk-shop of side-talks and general commentaries on the turn of events in the country.

'When a drunk starts anything, it is bound to be bizarre. The death of the primehead in this bizarre manner testifies to this.'

'How can soberness ride on drunkenness and not expect a bruise in the head?'

'Something started in the mouth can't end in the head. Things start in the head and end in the mouth, not the other way. How can madness start something and sanity will finish it?'

'We shall nevertheless try and I think the suicide theory is worth investigating.'

'People who commit suicide leave suicide notes. The primehead did not leave any.'

'It's not everyone that commits suicide that leaves a suicide note.'

'When the primehead's dead body was found, no one thought of suicide and suicide notes. The shock of his death and how he died were too shattering to allow for such a thought. Besides, it was getting dark. If there was a suicide note somewhere in the forest, we might not have seen it.'

'If there is a suicide note, it needs not be only in the forest. It can be somewhere in the primehead's palace or even in the pocket of the primehead's dress,' said the man sitting close to the deputy primehead's crony.

The chairman began wondering whether sitting arrangements in the primehead chambers were not according to political clans.

'To prove suicide, you don't even need a suicide note,' said the legal adviser. 'If the primehead shot himself, he must have shot himself with his own gun. In that case, the bullet hole in his head and the bullet in his head would be of his gun and not of some other gun.'

'That's a brilliant idea,' said the chairman. 'The only problem is that his gun cannot be found. I believe whoever killed him anticipated this brilliant idea and got rid of his gun. That his gun was not by his dead body is evidence enough that he did not commit suicide.'

There were murmurs of agreement with what the chairman had said.

'Unless of course someone removed his gun to make it look like murder,' said the deputy primehead's crony as the murmurs were dying down.

'And who may that someone be?' asked the chairman with an evil look on his face.

The deputy primehead's crony did not say anything. The atmosphere in the chambers has suddenly turned menacing.

'Without his gun to pursue the legal adviser's idea, we have to check and see if there is a suicide note,' said the organizing secretary, breaking the chilling silence.

The meeting was suspended for a while to conduct a search for a suicide note by the primehead. While the search was still going on, the chairman said, 'to even contemplate what we are doing now shows how much the spirit of the drunk is with us. It is shocking how reasonable people can suddenly lose their reason. Well...' he shrugged his shoulders and trailed away without completing what he wanted to say.

No suicide note was found in all the places they searched for it.

'We should not allow the world outside to know that when the primehead was shot dead, we thought of suicide and even went into the forest looking for a suicide note because the world will laugh at us,' the chairman said. 'Only a child can think the way we are thinking.'

'Since suicide is now ruled out, who killed the primehead?' the organizing secretary asked rhetorically.

'I have said a rioter might have broken into the jungle of Jonka Palace and shot him,' said the deputy primehead's crony, 'but no one wants to listen to me.'

'And I have said Jonka Palace is too fortified for that,' said the chairman.

'No place is too fortified to be broken into by a man with a determined mission,' said the crony.

'I think we should be allowed to please our every wandering fancy and indulge our every untenable thought,' said the chairman.

'But in the end, we will have to come to terms with the fact that this is an inside job. It is an inside *coup d'état*. But, let's nose around and see if we can find evidence of this improbable suggestion. '

To everyone's shock a tear was found somewhere in the wire fence of Jonka Palace.

'This proves nothing,' said the chairman, full of umbrage. 'This is no smoking gun. If it proves anything at all, it is that a rioter did not enter the Jonka jungle by the back fence and shot the primehead dead. Even if we had found the suicide note we were looking for, it won't have proved anything because the killer could leave such a note behind. It is the same thing with the tear on the fence.'

Surprisingly, even those who initially placed a lot of premium on a break on the fence of Jonka jungle seemed to have lost much of the premium they earlier placed on it now that a tear has been found in the fence. It was partly because of what the chairman had said and partly because it was searched for and found. If it was stumbled on accidentally, it would have generated a greater stir than it did when searched for and found.

'As far as I can see, the tear in the fence was made from inside the jungle and not from outside it.

It wasn't made by an outsider seeking to gain access into Jonka jungle, but by an insider within Jonka palace,' said the chairman, speaking rapidly. 'First, the fence wire bends inward which means it was from inside the fence was cut. If it was from outside, the fence wire would bend outward. Secondly, the only footsteps I can see outside the fence are those of a man walking away from the fence. There is no sign of footsteps walking towards the fence. This is where the killer has underplayed his hand. In these things, you either overplay or underplay your hand. You are either too sharp as to cut yourself or too blunt to cut anyone.'

The legal adviser was shocked by how quick the chairman's mind was taking in the situation. They were still looking at the tear in the fence, but the chairman had already gone beyond the fence to find footsteps walking away from the fence, but no footsteps walking towards the fence. For this, the chairman has earned his respect. It showed he had brains and was witty. Even if it turned out in the end that what he had just said was not true, he had shown he has the mind of an attorney.

Everyone could see that the fence wire was bent inward and not outward. But in the minds of some of the people, this did not necessarily mean the fence was torn from inside. There could still be an inward bent even if the cut was made from outside. Some of the people thinking this way expressed their feelings.

'Even though I know and you also know what you are saying is not true,' said the chairman, 'let's leave that issue for now and look outside the fence. What I see outside are the footsteps of a man walking away from the fence, but no footsteps that brought the man to the fence.'

Everyone looked outside the fence and could see what looked like the impressions of the footsteps of a man, but could not say if the impressions were the footsteps of a man walking away from the fence or towards it. It needed a closer look to determine that. They all went closer and looked and it seemed what the chairman was saying was true.

'Now it is turning out that it wasn't the primehead that committed suicide, but whoever killed him,' said the chairman full of zest. 'Well, until all our suspicions are allayed and puzzles resolved, no one can be sworn in as primehead. The chief archer should assume immediate leadership of the country. For now, let's focus on giving our departed primehead the decent burial he deserves.'

No one said anything either in support or opposition of what the chairman had said as they went back to the primehead's chambers.

Chapter Nineteen

Like most people in Bivan's house, Jamimi was gravely shocked and embarrassed by the bizarre and violent death of Merima and Boyama. To him, Bivan's house has been humiliated and disgraced by the indignities and crude tone of the primehead's death. The primehead of a country shot dead in the forest like a culled beast took all humor and politics out of him. It was a big smear that Bivan's house may not rub out or live down too fast.

'To think I was howling at men who were dead makes me feel wretched,' Jamimi said, feeling quite distraught. 'The shock of their death has shredded my nerves almost beyond repairs.'

'Let's not get sentimental,' said the party leader. 'This is not the moment for hysterics, but for soberness. The moment of hysteria is gone with the riots and the death of the primehead and Boyama. Now is a moment to get pragmatic. Let's think of how we might profit from their deaths rather than how we might have derided them in their death.'

'I wonder how you can be so coldly insensitive.'

'And I wonder how you can be so hysterically uncalculative. If I must be frank with you and myself, their deaths, particularly the death of Boyama, do not turn a hair in me,' said the party leader in a grating voice. 'Boyama lived despised by me and he has died unmourned by me. He does not matter a straw to me now as he has always.'

'You are intensely heartless.'

'And extensively selfish too, you should not forget to add. Perhaps, you have only heard about poverty. I have lived with it, through it and in it. Perhaps, poverty has only whispered to you. When I was born, the first thing that shouted at me was poverty. One thing that poverty teaches you is never to allow your heart to think for you, but your stomach. Right now, it is my stomach thinking for me.'

'I hand to you the laureate of heartlessness. But I tell you, you will not drag me to your level of callousness.'

'Life is comic if you see it for what it is - a farce. It is tragic if you see it for what it is not - a pleasure. I see life for what it is and that is why very few things shock me.'

'What do you think the UAC potentates would do now that both the primehead and Boyama are dead?' Mengo more inclined to the disposition of the party leader asked the party leader.

'I can't say,' said the party leader. 'But you know they are Godless people. They will not see in what happened the hand of God and be charitable in their hearts. Instead, they would want to hang on to power by the crude and evil ways they have been hanging onto it.'

'So, the deputy primehead will now become the primehead. That would be very terrible for Bivan's house,' said Talgon. 'The deputy primehead became deputy primehead shortly after his apprenticeship with the devil.'

'From what I know of the UAC chairman, he would not sit tamely by and watch the deputy primehead become primehead. He would fight him to a standstill if not to the grave. This is where our hope lies. UAC will implode.'

'The deputy primehead no doubt is both a bad influence and a nightmare even to his party apparatchiks. I will not be surprised if UAC implodes because of resentment to his ascension to the office of primehead,' said Jamimi.

'I can see the fierce struggles in your mind to take to me,' said the party leader.

'We will do well if we don't deride each other,' said Jamimi.

'Right now, Jonka Palace is vacant. Any man of valor can walk into it and declare himself primehead,' said the party leader.

'It is not as vacant as you think. The deputy primehead is there looking gloatingly at it. You have to clear him on your way to that seat. I can tell you that this is something you will not find easy,' said Jamimi.

'If only the rioters had not been chilled or appeased by the deaths of Boyama and the primehead, we would have mobilized them and marched on Jonka Palace,' said Mengo.

'I would have been glad to see such new fire in you,' said the party leader.

While they were still talking, the musical countdown to BBC news began chiming. They froze to attention. To their shock, among the news headlines was the arrest of the deputy primehead for masterminding the assassination of the primehead.

'This is something,' Jamimi muttered.

'The deputy primehead's chickens are coming home to roost,' said the party leader, excitement chattering in his head like the canaries of Longo country

'The times are truly turbulent and pleasing,' said Mengo. 'This is more than the rough and tumble of politics. But I thought under the constitution the deputy primehead enjoys immunity.'

'Not against a charge of treason which he appears to be facing now,' said Jamimi. 'Against treason there is no immunity.'

'What is the punishment for treason under the law?' asked Mengo.

'Death by hanging,' said Jamimi. 'You will be hanged by the neck until you die while a priest prays for the repose of your soul.'

'That is if your soul is able to free itself from the rope that has snuffed out your life,' said the party leader. 'Ah Jalleh, consort of the whore of the sovereign. The whore has finally betrayed you to the philistines.' For a while he was silent before he continued excitedly. 'I told you! 'I told you the UAC chairman will cook the deputy primehead's goose. But even I did not think he would cook it so fast and in such a big pot. Ahh … UAC! sharing death equally! I believe in the great beyond you will be sharing decay and worms equally.'

'But what evidence do you think the chairman and those supporting him would have found within such a short time to cause the arrest of the deputy primehead on such grave allegation?'

'How would I know?' said the party leader. 'What we all know is that he is hated by the chairman and other party potentates for his treachery and megalomaniac tendencies. The primehead killed the way he was makes him the prime suspect.'

'Things can be funny,' said Mengo. 'Instead of becoming primehead he has become prime suspect.'

'He is still primehead, but only for the hangman's noose,' said the party leader, sarcastically.

'The chairman of UAC is himself not a good man,' said Jamimi.

'In my village we have a saying that *when a bastard climbs a tree, it is another bastard that is sent to bring him down*. The chairman is the bastard that can bring the deputy primehead down from the tree he is on,' said the party leader.

'What I don't understand is why good men like good men, but bad men do not like bad men,' said Mengo.

'Bad men can only prey on good men,' said Talgon. 'How can a hyena be excited over the replacement of sheep with wolves?'

'We are supposed to be an independent, sovereign nation. But we are so dumb that we can't even talk to ourselves,' said Jamimi. 'It takes the voice of our colonial master for us to hear an important news like this. It is very bad.'

'People are inside a room; but it is someone outside the room that is telling those inside what is happening inside the room,' said Mengo. 'It's both ridiculous and irritable.'

'You can always be sure that England will always be in this country than you can ever hope to be in it and knows it than you can ever hope to know it,' said the party leader, yawning.

Chapter Twenty

The deputy primehead was arraigned in court four days after the death of the primehead. But it took the caretaker government of Waddo more than two months to start bringing witnesses to prove the charges of murder and treason preferred against the deputy primehead. Waddo aware that whatever was the outcome of the case after its conclusion he would have to leave office was not keen on the speedy prosecution of the case. If the deputy primehead was convicted for the alleged offences, a new election had to be organized and conducted for a new primehead and deputy primehead. This would take time and Waddo's caretaker government would stay in power. If on the other hand the deputy primehead was discharged and acquitted at the end of the case, he immediately assumed office as the primehead. This meant the tenure of Waddo as the head of the caretaker government would only be as long as the case lasted in court. To ensure he got a conviction and thereby prolong the tenure of his caretaker government, he engaged the services of a seasoned private legal practitioner to take over the prosecution of the case from the Attorney General who filed the case. He had little or no faith in the ability of the Attorney General and his band of unserious and untested lawyers to get the conviction he so much needed in the case. But he had a lot of confidence in the ability of the private legal practitioner he engaged to deliver to him the head of the deputy primehead. For now, he was the occupant of Jonka Palace and therefore the storekeeper of the mountain of wild fleece. He would stay as long as he could and get as much as he could from the mountain of wild fleece.

'Bivan's house! Whoever ascends the mountain of wild fleece does not want to come down,' said Mengo. 'Everyone seemed to want to be buried up there as if being buried up there is a visa to heaven.'

'And so it is,' said the party leader. 'On the mountain of wild fleece what you see is heaven. Down the mountain what you see is hell. Therefore those on the mountain are sieged by fears of the hell below the mountain.'

'They are sieged by a hell they created you should add,' said Jamimi. 'There would have been no hell down the mountain if those on the mountain had been allowing fleece falling on the mountain to go downhill. Rain falling on the mountain is not allowed to trickle downhill and so there is drought and famine downhill. Those on the mountain of wild fleece who catch up all the rain uphill are quick to forget they ascended the mountain from downhill and there they shall return. When it is time to return and they look down and see the hell below, they don't want to return. But they must return. The constitution is a rope around the necks of all those who climb the mountain of wild fleece. Whoever would not come down on his own when his time was done, would be pulled down by the rope of the constitution.'

'You know in the village in the evening when goats with leashes around their necks are taken home for the night after a day-long grazing in the bush, a glutton goat still flicking its tongue for fodder often had to be dragged by its leash home. That's how governments in Bivan's house are behaving,' said Mengo

'It is bad to have to be pulled away like a goat that does not know when it should say farewell to the pasture and go home to chew the cud,' said Jamimi with a deep sigh.

'The unfortunate thing about Waddo is that there is no leash around his neck. He has no term of office,' said Mengo.

'It may seem there is no leash around his neck, but I can tell you there is a very long leash around his neck that would pluck him down when the sun is setting,' Jamimi said in a voice free of his earlier weariness.

'What is this long leash?' Mengo asked.

'The people's resentment,' Jamimi said. 'The people now know they are not as powerless as they earlier thought. They now know they can remove from their sight what they don't want to see. So they will remove Waddo from their sight when he becomes an eyesore.'

It was in the court the second revolt erupted. If Jamimi was in court, it would have been said he engineered it or at least that his presence did. But Jamimi was not in court. However, Waddo was in court. The deputy primehead was to give evidence in his defense that day and Waddo who since the case started had never been in court wanted to be in court to shore up the performance of his lawyer. From reports he had being receiving on the progress of the case in court, he hadn't been too impressed with the way the case was going. It looked like the deputy primehead would get an acquittal at the end of the case and he dreaded that outcome. Apart from not wanting to vacate the office of head of the caretaker government fast, he was afraid of what the deputy primehead would do to him when he assumed office as primehead. Apart from being the one prosecuting the deputy primehead, he had made a number of derogatory remarks on the person of the deputy primehead and he knew the latter to be a very vindictive man who would stop at nothing to hit back at him. Hitting back at him would be the easiest thing given how much he had stolen from government coffers during the short time he had spent in office. Rather than allow the deputy primehead seize the reins of office from him, he would find a way of eliminating him if he was convinced he would be acquitted by the court. But he might end up in exactly the same situation the deputy primehead was. No, there must be some other way. He had tried purchasing the judgment, but it seemed the deputy primehead who was a big-time smuggler and had a lot of money before joining politics had also being seeing the judge with a lot of money and so the judge had remained non-committal to him. But there was something the judge was doing that was pleasing to him. The judge receiving money from both parties seemed to be delaying the case so that he would continue to feather his nest from this plum case. Waddo appreciated this attitude of the judge. It was giving to him with the left hand what the judge was withholding from him with the right. Still, he was not happy with the way the case was going. The deputy primehead was a big scare to him. Today that he was testifying Waddo could not resist the urge to be in court in person to take stock of the situation himself. But if he had known he would not return to Jonka palace as the head of the caretaker government, perhaps no urge would have moved him to the court that day. If he also knew that his presence in court would so spark off the brilliance of the lawyer he engaged to handle the case in the catastrophic manner he did, perhaps he would not have attended the court that day or perhaps he wouldn't have even engaged the lawyer in the first place.

Given the pressure Waddo was piling on him since he started the prosecution of the case, Gomkano the lawyer had always known that one day Waddo would want to come to court to witness proceedings in the matter. That day he suspected to be the day the deputy primehead would testify in his defense. Because he suspected this would happen, he had prepared himself before it happened. He wanted to enact on that day a court drama that had never been witnessed in the annals of court litigation in Bivan's house. There were documents he would have tendered through his own witnesses, but deliberately withheld them so that he would confront the deputy primehead with them when he was called by his lawyer to defend himself.

Unknown to many people, Gomkano was an alcoholic. By nature, he was a very shy person. He therefore needed the tonic of alcohol to perform well in court. So, every morning before going to court, he took a small glass of whiskey to charge him with the confidence he needed and the eloquence alcohol always gave him. On unlucky days when the court did not sit early or when there were more senior lawyers in the court who would have to call their cases before him, the effect of the whiskey on him would have totally worn out when his case was called.

Then he would not put up the superlative performance he was known for. To prevent this from happening, he carried some whiskey with him to court. If there was a delay in his case being called, he found a hidden place and took a shot of whiskey shortly before his case was called.

On the day the deputy primehead was to testify, after taking a glass and a half of whiskey, Gomkano put a little bottle of whiskey in his bag before heading to court, his team of lawyers in tow. As if invisible forces were at work in his favor that day, the whiskey was beginning to take its much-needed effect when it was time for him to begin his cross-examination of the deputy primehead.

He stood up and adjusted his wig and gown. This was always his ritual whenever he stood up to perform a task in court. He would adjust his wig first before the gown. Today he performed this ritual with more ceremony than he was wont to. He cleared his throat and focused his eyes on the deputy primehead.

'What was the relationship between you and the primehead like before he met his death?' Gomkano began his cross-examination.

'Cordial,' said the deputy primehead with an unfriendly look on his face.

'Is it true that in the last cabinet meeting before the primehead met his death, he complained bitterly that you have not been forthcoming in helping him quell the riots and demonstration sweeping through the country then?'

'That's not true,' the deputy primehead said, his face looking like faeces that had been stepped on.

'We shall see about that,' murmured Gomkano. 'Do you know Chawak?' he continued his cross-examination.

'You mean my security aide?'

'Yes, your security aide.'

'Of, course I know him. What is the matter with him?'

'Nothing.'

'For how long have you known Chawak?'

'Since I joined politics, we have been together.'

'If you see Chawak, will you be able to recognize him?'

'What sort of ridiculous question is that?' fumed the deputy primehead. 'I will not answer this question.'

The defense lawyer stood up to say the question was not only ridiculous, but

irrelevant and should not be asked. The time
of the court was being wasted.

'It's for the court to say whether its time
is being wasted or not,' replied Gomkano. 'It's
also the court that can say whether a question
is relevant or not. I insist on this question
being answered.'

The court told him to go on and he
repeated the question to the deputy
primehead.

'Yes, if I see him, I can recognize him.'

Chawak who was sitting in the court
was asked to stand up and he stood up.

'Is that Chawak?'

'Yes.'

'In the UAC primaries, you contested
against the deceased primehead and lost.'

'Yes.'

'There is no love lost between you
and the chairman of your party.'

'What did you say?'

'I said you and the chairman of your
party do not like each other.'

'I am not aware of that.'

'He didn't support you during the UAC
primaries. He supported the deceased
primehead.'

'I don't know about that.'

'He also opposed your being picked as a running mate to the primehead.'

'I am hearing that from you.'

'The reason the chairman didn't want you either as primehead candidate or running mate is that you were once in PLM and was even its caretaker chairman at some point, but you later jumped ship and joined the UAC. He sees you as a turncoat, an opportunist who can betray the UAC if that would serve your interest.'

'Yes, I was in the PLM. But it's not true that the UAC chairman distrust me because I later left the PLM.'

'The chairman of UAC is very powerful in the party.'

'That's true.'

'You lobbied him for his support.'

'Every candidate did. It wasn't just me.'

'If the chairman does not support a candidate for a position, the candidate can hardly get it.'

'That's not true.'

'If it's not true why did you lobby him for his support?'

There was no answer from the deputy primehead.

'Did the chairman eventually support you for the office of running mate?'

'Yes, he did.'

'To get the UAC chairman to support your nomination as running mate, you had to make an undertaking to undermine your former party the PLM which looked set to win the election with Jamimi as its primehead candidate.'

'That's not true, that's not true!' the deputy primehead who before now had comported himself well, cried. 'You have no proof of what you are saying.'

'I have,' said Gomkano.

Gomkano sought the leave of the court to allow him bring in a television set, video machine and cassettes into the court to play some cassettes that would prove his allegations. The defense lawyer objected, but was overruled by the court. The television set, video machine and cassettes were brought into the court from Gomkano's car and played. The first cassette showed the primehead in a cabinet meeting in Jonka Palace with all his ministers and the deputy primehead. When the cassette came to the relevant portion of Gomkano's cross-examination, the primehead was seen and heard telling the deputy primehead that he is constrained to complain to the cabinet on how when asked by the primehead to go and discuss with different interest groups and personalities who could help quell the riots, the deputy primehead had refused to do so.'

'Now, is it true that in the last cabinet meeting before the primehead met his death, he complained bitterly that you have not been forthcoming in helping him quell the riots and demonstrations sweeping through the country then?'

'It's true.'

Gomkano inserted another cassette into the video machine. In this cassette Chawak was seen with three people pulling off a rail bar from the railtrack in a very thick forest.

'Now is it true you sent Chawak to remove a rail bar from the railtrack to derail the PLM campaign train?' Gomkano asked, his attention back to the deputy primehead.

Again, the lawyer for the defense objected saying the cassette was a film trick. But when he turned and saw the look of guilt on the face of the deputy primehead, he faltered in his speech. The judge was also looking at the deputy primehead. The quilt on his face was more eloquent than if he had gone verbal with it.

'Well, counsel,' the judge murmured.

The defense lawyer mumbled some inaudible words, shrugged his shoulders and sat down. In the public gallery there were swearing of oaths and violent curses on the deputy primehead.

'Do you think the primehead was murdered or he committed suicide as some people had suggested?' Gomkano continued his cross-examination.

'How would I know? I wasn't where he died.'

'I am not saying you were there. But like everyone else, you must hold an opinion on whether he was killed or he committed suicide. For example, some newspapers hold the opinion that he committed suicide.'

'Well, you know he died after Boyama was killed. If he heard of Boyama's death, the shock of it might drive him to commit suicide.'

'But I hold a different opinion. My opinion is that he was killed and you killed him and I have proof of it,' Gomkano said, taking his eyes from the deputy primehead and fixing them on the television set that was still in the courtroom.

The impact of this statement on the deputy primehead was devastating. He was punchdrunk. When his eyes fell on the television, his condition seemed to deteriorate. From this television, two damning evidences had flowed. How was he to know a third would not flow from it? The television seemed to be having a worse effect on him than what Gomkano had said. It was now looking like a hangman slipping the noose round his neck. It was now looking like a rattle snake rearing to strike. But he would not go down alone. He would go down with the chairman of the UAC and Waddo the head of the caretaker government. He had no proof they supplied Gomkano with the evidences he was using to decimate him, but they were both sitting in court and from the expressions on their faces, they were enjoying what was happening to him. He would make sure he did not go down alone. They will go down with him. From the curses and swearing he heard coming from the public gallery, he knew he would hardly leave the courtroom alive. Outside the courtroom, he could see a sea of people who because of lack of space in the courtroom were standing outside. The court was under siege. Like those inside the courtroom, people outside the courtroom had also been swearing and cursing him. The spirit of the drunk was still alive in Bivan's house he thought. He could feel it even in the courtroom. Gomkano in the course of his cross-examination had moved closer to him and he had smelled beer in him. He now suspected the lawyer to be on riot against him. No, he would not come out of this alive, now that he was convinced the lawyer was going to play a film showing Chawak shooting the primehead. In a way, holding his trial while the spirit of riot was still abroad was unfair because it guaranteed his death; in a way, it was fair because it guaranteed the death of anyone he chose to implicate. Yes, he would not go down alone.

Gomkano was watching him closely. 'My lord, I humbly apply for leave to play another cassette that will prove to your lordship the accused killed the primehead,' he said, pulling another cassette from his bag.

Before the judge could say anything, the deputy primehead screamed, 'yes, I killed him! He deserved to die. He wanted to have me impeached by the archers, to have me shot down before my time was off. But I didn't kill him alone. The chairman of UAC and Waddo the head of the caretaker government were also involved in the plot to kill him.'

Gomkano smiled to himself. His trick has worked as he hoped it would. The cassette was a hoax. It contains nothing incriminating the deputy primehead.

Like the deputy primehead had hoped, the UAC chairman and the head of the caretaker

government shared death with him in the court
premises that day.

Chapter Twenty-One

While the UAC chairman never trusted the deputy primehead, the primehead who the chairman always said was a babe in the woods did, at least before the riots broke out. Believing the deputy primehead to be a snake who could strike anyone anytime, the chairman had him watched from the day he endorsed him as running mate to Merima. He must have something he would use against him if he turned against him. When he insisted on an undertaking by the deputy primehead before he endorsed him as running mate, he did so deliberately knowing the deputy primehead desperate for power would accept to do something criminal that he might later use against him. It was he who suggested the derailment of the PLM train. Even though he believed the deputy primehead to be without scruples, he was nonetheless shocked that he acceded to his suggestion without a second thought. He had told his spy to make sure that whoever the deputy primehead employed to cause the derailment of the train was filmed while executing his assignment and the spy did so. The same spy filmed the cabinet meeting. But somehow his filming devices which he was always planting along the paths of the deputy primehead and his agents were not where the primehead was killed and so the chairman had no evidence that the deputy primehead murdered the primehead. He was very angry with his spy, but there was nothing he could do.

Part of the reason he was gathering adverse evidences against the deputy primehead was for the good of the primehead who he felt was too naïve and totally lacking the wiliness and guile needed to navigate the murky and treacherous political waters of Bivan's house. Now that the primehead had been claimed by a crocodile in the hazardous waters of politics and he strongly suspected the deputy primehead to be that crocodile, he decided to use what he had to see if it would scorch the head of the serpent that had smitten his friend to death. So he turned the films over to Gomkano and his gambit had paid off. But not without his own head rolling along that of the deputy primehead.

'Death to the deputy primehead, death to the UAC chairman and death to Waddo the head of the caretaker government!' the crowd in the public gallery and outside the courtroom chanted. 'Death to any policeman that with his gun or baton, says live to any of these oppressors! Long live Jamimi! Long live Bivan's house!'

The judge sensing trouble, without saying a word, slipped into his chambers behind him. His orderly on his heels slammed the door close behind them as the crowd charged forward.

The security operatives that came with Waddo and those that brought the deputy primehead to court from prison opened fire on the crowd, but were soon swallowed up by the crowd. Their guns were seized and used by the crowd first to shoot them and then those they sought to protect.

In his death throes, the deputy primehead slobbered, 'a … bo…ttle of beer should re…place the ti…ger in our code of arms. To it we owe the new fight in us.'

You have said something there,' someone said. 'Please, someone should take this money and buy a carton of star or gulder for us from Madam Outside over there.' He brought out a wad of money from his back pocket, counted a few notes and gave to a lad that came forward to run his errand.

The lad dashed off with the money and was soon back with a carton of star. He only succeeded in taking a bottle to the man who sent him. The rest were plucked off the carton as he was carrying it to the buyer. It was when he apprehended that he might end up taking an empty carton to the buyer that he took hold of a bottle and let go the carton still containing about two bottles.

On receiving the bottle, the person who sent for the beer, using his teeth, flicked off the cap and took a long swig.

'Cheers to the spirit of Benbendo!' he cried, holding the half empty bottle of star up in the air.

'Cheers! Cheers! cheers!' chanted other people with bottles of star in their hands held up in the air. Even those without bottles raised their clenched fists in the air in a wayward salute.

'From being a cemetery, the graveyard of Africa, Bivan's house is now a theatre where dramas of all sorts take place. All thanks to Benbendo!'

'Mobocracy will guide democracy in Bivan's house.'

'Cheers to the bottle!'

'Cheers to Jamimi the new primehead of Bivan's house.'

'Cheers! Cheers! cheers!' the crowd cried.'

Jamimi was made primehead on the street.

A year later, the party leader said to the primehead, 'this is a whole lot of bad country. I can't see anyone in this country good enough to succeed you.'

'True,' said Mengo. 'Almost everyone in this country is wet and dirty with corruption. We are all like farmers coming back from the farm in the rain with all the dirt of the earth. There is no one as clean as His Excellency to sit on this seat without soiling it.'

'Farmers are hardworking, decent folks,' said
the party leader. 'I will rather say, we look like the
pig from the village muddy pond or something the
cat brought in.'

'Whatever,' quipped Mengo. 'There is no one
clean enough to succeed the primehead.

'Well, I don't know about that,' said Jamimi.
'But let me hear the people.'

'We are the people,' said the party leader.

"It's so hard to see …' murmured Jamimi. 'But
what I am hearing is opening my eyes to see what I
can't see.'